THE GREAT CYPRUS

THINK TANK

THE GREAT CYPRUS THINK TANK

a novel

Larry Lockridge

IGUANA

Publisher: Meghan Behse
Editor: Paula Chiarcos
Cover design and drawings: © Marcia Scanlon 2020

ISBN 978-1-77180-424-0 (hardcover)
ISBN 978-1-77180-337-3 (paperback)
ISBN 978-1-77180-338-0 (epub)

This is an original print edition of *The Great Cyprus Think Tank*.

to my sister Jeanne,
source of joy and light

CONTENTS

PROLOGUE

Whenever my dreamworld turns bleak, I glare at my writing desk and cry out to solitary walls, "I'll go abroad!" In early 2022 I was no longer dreaming of sphinxes, pyramids, and caravansaries. My night fantasies had given way to dark frustrations. I couldn't find my classroom and, when I did, was without a syllabus or anything to say, while nameless students peered into iPhones and sullenly drifted off. When I took the elegant stairwell to my gala book launch at the Century Club, I beheld old friends no longer recognizable, for this was our fortieth high school reunion, and I was the emcee. A porter on the Trans Canada told me the Rockies had been leveled because—didn't I know?—Saskatchewan was the new look for Canada. My worst dream was to survey my image in the bathroom mirror and see that I was sixty-two—worst because upon awakening I sighed at its unnerving truth.

The mind beneath mind that is the wellspring of dreams needed fresh water, and I knew where to find it—in the fabled and parched isle of Cyprus.

My doctorate in sociolinguistics has taught me a nonacademic kind of writer's life. I pack my bags and set up in an exotic locale, quickly learn the language and native customs, and within a year or two, produce a novelistic memoir. You may already have read some of them. Thanks for downloading another—Bart Beasley's *The Great Cyprus Think Tank*.

I was born in 1960 in Ottawa but spent four years in Cyprus while my father, a minor Canadian diplomat stationed in Nicosia in 1970, did what he could to make amends for the earlier British occupation of that unfortunate island. He advised the UN Peace Keeping Force in its deployment of Canadian military fodder. Upon the Turkish invasion of 1974 he took credit for deceiving the Turks and protecting the airport in Nicosia by telling the Canadians to move their pitiable handful of tanks around all night as noisily as possible, with bright lights. Good thinking. The Turks concluded the airport was too heavily fortified to bother with, at least at the time. But the invasion was so stressful that my father suffered a mild coronary and was sent home to Ottawa along with his wife and me, their only child. He died not long after.

Having clocked the years from ten to fourteen there, I found that Cyprus had lodged deep in my memory cells and re-emerged from time to time as a yearning. In 2022 it beckoned again.

As you know, to the amazement of everybody the world over, the island was reunified earlier that year. In a new pan-Cypriot bi-communal federation, restrictions on travel across the border imposed by the Turks in 1974 were lifted. Resettlement of displaced Greek Cypriots and Turkish Cypriots was soon underway, with somewhat less gory jousting over old homesteads than might have been expected. But ethnic animosities persisted, as did other worries—desertification, a diet dominated by British chips, a rising sea level that threatened hatcheries of the famed sea turtles, the slaughter of migratory songbirds, and looting of antiquities for sale on the black market.

I'm not by nature a social engineer or utopianist. One motive was frankly self-interest in whipping up fresh material for this memoir. But I'd also felt at times an urge to do my species some good beyond fictionalized memoirs that leave little trace beyond an evening's frolic in the minds of a handful of pale, unsatisfied readers seeking ports of call they can never visit because too poor, infirm, or lazy. Then too, there were deficits in my life that prompted my conscience to acts of compensation.

I applied to the Soros foundation to fund a think tank. Let me enlist specialists to rescue the island, I told them. It took only a few hours on the internet to seek out the world's finest, some of them already familiar with the island, and add their names to the application form. They included a zoologist, a nutritionist, a meteorologist, a neurologist, and an archeologist. My project may smack of presumptuous American world-beating, but keep in mind that I'm Canadian.

The Soros foundation knew a good idea when it saw one and, within weeks, was depositing large sums in my checking account at Chase on lower Broadway. This wasn't my money, but it felt good to see my account plump up beyond a midlist author's best imagining. I was teaching creative nonfiction at NYU as an adjunct and barely paying rent for a modest one-bedroom at 68 Carmine Street.

I'll spare you two years of logistics. The Cyprus Think Tank took up residence in Káthikas, a small village in the west overlooking ancient Páphos. We numbered five geniuses plus me.

You may already know us from the singular episodes we occasioned during our brief tenure on the island, having gained influence within the new pan-Cypriot government. The Minister of the Interior was amused by my scheme, viewing it as crackbrained but harmless enough. And she was happy to receive a handsome subsidy from Soros, which could have purchased the entire island with cash on hand.

My special interest in Cyprus, beyond saving it and writing this memoir, was the literary connections—not native writers but the outsiders Arthur Rimbaud and Lawrence Durrell, who lived for brief spells on the island. The French poet was the negative lure, Durrell the positive. Rimbaud gave up verse at the age of twenty as the most precocious writer in the history of literature. He turned his back on the whole enterprise. What boots it? Whenever I suffer writer's block, I say to myself, *Rimbaud knew he need not write more, so why should I?* Durrell kept writing beyond *The Alexandria Quartet*, but never again so well.

I had good reason to believe that Rimbaud left a notebook on Cyprus. I wanted that notebook, I wanted it! And I wanted to visit Béllapais in the North where Durrell had lived, thinking his shade might breathe words into me. I needed them.

Another lure was William Shakespeare, most of whose *Othello* is set in Cyprus, probably Famagusta. I couldn't know early on how much this tragic drama would impinge on my farce.

In its contradictions Cyprus is a haunting enigma. Yes, it has everything—from splendid antiquities of the many cultures that have flourished there, to an enchanted geography of mountains, deserts, and beaches, to legendary cities, monasteries, mosques, and castles, to the celebrated haloumi cheese and zivanía brandy. But it suffers the worst consequences of climate change, the ethnic enmities that have spilt kraters of blood and still simmer here and there, the loathsome residue of rapacious mining and industry, the public-health menace of a greasy British diet, and the geopolitical disadvantage of proximity to both the Middle East and Africa, a pawn caught in the interplay of larger powers. It's not much of a stretch to say that in Cyprus we find Planet Earth in miniature. After the ordeals of Brexit, with its improbable focus on a 310-mile internal Irish border, and the coronavirus pandemic, with its promiscuous feasting on a 24,901-mile ring of hapless humans, I feel it's time to return Cyprus to the map of global awareness. If you stick with my memoir, you'll be getting a parable of the human race in the early twenty-first century for ninety-nine cents.

And I promise you adventures I couldn't have made up, including dark forces intent on sabotaging my benevolent scheme. I admit to having little imagination but do have a memoirist's habit of jotting everything down at day's end. If you doubt my reliability, I've taken inspiration from Rimbaud and have tucked my own notebook somewhere in the vast library of the Oneida Community Mansion

House in upstate New York, where my story ends and where I wrote this memoir over a period of three weeks. If you find my notebook, read it and decide for yourself whether I have exaggerated. But the staff doesn't permit removal of anything from their library, even for private reading in one of their rental rooms. A ghostly impersonator of the Oneida Community founder, John Humphrey Noyes, will track down and bring to justice anybody who violates this rule. Unless you relish confronting a religious lunatic, I'd advise you to let my notebook rest unmolested among the relics of print culture that gather dust in the stately Mansion House left by the polyamorous utopians, who remind us that utopias come but mostly go.

Chapter One

AT THE TAVERNA

The evening of April 1, 2024, four members of our think tank converged on Taverna Imoyeni, the finest eatery in Káthikas, where I had placed an order for a twenty-four-plate meze, good ploy for quick conviviality and proven remedy for jet lag. Our archeologist, Melusina Frei, was delayed by a strike of her fourteen sea divers, and our neurologist, Albert Vygotsky, was arrested when taken for a terrorist at the Athens airport. The houses of those who arrived were well-stocked with zivanía. When we hobbled into the taverna, it was clear we had all a drop taken of the island's famed white brandy.

We quickly turned our conversation to matters of substance, as befits a think tank, but it's not a good idea to talk politics when drunk and sitting down to meze surrounded by strangers. Darcy Peatman, our English zoologist, was short on this etiquette. "The truth about this island is that the Turkish Cypriots were right to be spooked in 1974. That bloody war criminal Kissinger wanted to follow up on his triumph in Chile—why not destroy Cyprus?"

"A track record sort of thing?" asked our nutritionist, Jasmine Ivory, sitting across from Darcy and monitoring him as one might a live lobster.

Darcy practiced vegetarianism and scooped up local animals wherever he traveled. Our rented domiciles would soon be full of stray cats to keep snakes at bay. Wearing safari clothing that resembled Stewart Granger's in *King Solomon's Mines*, he was a devotee of zoologist Gerald Durrell, younger brother of Lawrence. His graying walrus mustache, lively jowls, and combative personality went before him through many viral YouTube videos where he could be seen hand-smacking at rapacious hunters, indifferent zookeepers, and sadistic children pulling tails of dogs, cats, and lemurs. On Cyprus he had already intervened at Cape Lára, rescuing sea turtles from tourists. He was happy to return to rescue migratory songbirds—the locals pickled and ate millions of them. Also the mouflon, the great-horned sheep that had almost disappeared into stew in the nineteenth century. These admirable passions, when redirected to world politics, prompted even the sympathetic to wish he'd keep his fucking voice down.

"Right you are," replied Darcy. "Kissinger and the CIA gave the Greek junta the green light to oust Makarios. A good man was replaced by Nikos Sampson. The creep shot Turkish Cypriots for sport, got himself photographed standing on one as a trophy. Anybody want to see the photo?" Silence. "No wonder Turkey invited itself down to lend a hand to its own. Not that I liked the invasion or the Turks. Those blackguards bumped off thousands of Brits at Gallipoli."

"Come on, Darcy," said our meteorologist, Gayle Drake-Larkin, raising her voice to match his. "Turkey was just waiting for a pretext to invade, and Kissinger was happy to serve it up. Way to go, Henry. But that invasion was hardly justified, you know. Thousands died for no reason at all, thousands were displaced. And Kissinger was a snake. A large cat should have eaten him. Turkey had strategic military bases dear to Henry's heart. He saw to it that the Greek Cypriots would get their gooses cooked."

I'll not break in here with a history lesson, telling you all about Archbishop Makarios, for instance. It's complicated. Look it up on Wikipedia under "History of Cyprus since 1878," if you like. For now, just keep in mind that the 1974 invasion resulted in the

Turkish occupation of one-third of the island and its de facto partition, with severe dislocation of Greek and Turkish Cypriots alike. Nicosia became a divided city with a hideous wall you'd climb over at your peril. The sole issue the world's governments agreed on was that the Turkish occupation wasn't legal. Only Turkey thought otherwise and gave its self-created zone full diplomatic recognition. Anything circular about this?

"Shouldn't that be *geese*?" asked Jasmine. "I can do a first-rate goose, or geese, for that matter." She was trying to change the subject. It's unseemly to bring up the Turkish invasion, and some of our neighboring diners knew enough English to stare at us. One party asked for another table.

"Any way you look at it," continued Gayle, "that invasion was a bummer."

"Yeah, I agree, a bummer," said Darcy, pulling in his sails. "Just because a few Turkish Cypriots were being offed was no excuse for human wave attacks. The wildlife in the North went underground. Animals know when it's time to head for cover. Same thing happened after your presidential election in 2016. The long-eared myotis bats were terrified of Trump and holed up in their tree cavities . . . No, I'm not kidding!"

"Don't leave your island out of the picture," cautioned Gayle, pushing up her Snoopy hat. "If there hadn't been a British occupation for eighty years, no Turkish invasion down the road. You Brits taxed the poor Cypriots to death to pay off a stupid debt to a sultan, and what you did to their agriculture really sucked. That's just for starters."

Maybe carrying a degree of British guilt over Cyprus, Darcy conceded with a grunt and grinned. They were having a tiff but he seemed to like Gayle. You get a gaggle of geniuses together at your peril. I hoped they would get along.

Twenty years earlier, Gayle had worked as a precocious teenager with Al Gore on *An Inconvenient Truth* and was savvy about politics. Adjunct professor of Atmospheric Science at the

University of California, Davis, she didn't wish to be tied down by an academic career. Was a reckless overachiever who performed in air shows, doing upside-down figure eights and terrifying nosedives in a rehabilitated World War II Grumman F8F Bearcat fighter. She earned extra cash as a skywriter. New to Cyprus, she was eager to do something about the desertification that forced the humiliated Cypriots to buy secondhand water from Greece, itself parched.

"You Brits left two legacies," said Jasmine. "Driving on the wrong side of the road and fries—I mean *chips* as you Brits call them. Waiter, please remove the chips!"

Michalis skulked away with four platefuls, and Darcy looked aggrieved. These were the first of many mezes Jasmine waved away that evening. With dishes she allowed, she took ample portions but played with them more than she ate them, tucking one piece of food under another.

"I'll hound the Minister of the Interior again about chips. Have you looked at the Cypriot waistline? It's that ancient Venus figurine all over again, really fat."

"Jasmine," I said diplomatically, "could I suggest that you not knock Venus after Melusina arrives. Her career hangs on finding Venus—you know, Aphrodite."

"I hope the marble Aphrodite gives Cypriot women a new aesthetic. Their husbands might spend less time at tavernas, more in thalami . . . What do *you* think, Darcy?"

There was a hint of flirtation in Jasmine's question—that reference to Greek bedrooms and a certain lilt in her voice—but Darcy was too much in a funk over chips to notice. He sighed.

"Sorry to send your chips away, Darcy," said Jasmine, "but face it, they're cooked in lard and hardly vegetarian."

He again conceded the point with a grunt, adding, "This island is tough going for the likes of me, but it's too bloody hot for carnivores. No sense stuffing yourself with *kléftigo, pastourmás, gourorunópoulo,* and *lougánigo* if you're being broiled by the sirocco!"

Jasmine laughed and was clearly warming to Darcy and his brash energy—the first upsurge of romantic currents that will unsettle my story.

"I'm with you there, dude," she said. "One crusade of mine is to get the locals to eat more *glystrida*, *rókka*, and taro root. Also *koliandro* sprigs."

"Please call it a *mission*, Jasmine," I put in. "You've been here twice before. Cypriots aren't keen on *crusades*. Remember Richard the Lionheart took umbrage over how his sister and fiancée were treated by the Byzantine prince and plundered the whole island. Sold it as a down payment to the Knights Templar. Same knights taxed the surviving Cypriots to pay the balance and cut the heads off resistant taxpayers. Thousands of heads. A fine piece of work, that first crusade. The others weren't any better."

"I draw the line at *glystrida*," said Darcy, "but the other inedibles I'm willing to eat. One crusade—er, *mission*—of mine is to rescue the *ambelopoúlia*, poor bloody beasties."

"I'm with you there," said Jasmine eagerly. "Let's conspire on this. There are other ways the Cypriots can get their protein. Problem is that pickled songbirds are so tasty, so I hear. Byron loved the Italian version, *beccaficos*. No conscience. But I love Lord Byron. You Brits produced some knockout poets."

Growing up Black in a white Georgetown community, Jasmine didn't confront chitlins and deep-fried chicken, but she studied nutrition at Indiana University and was appalled by the Hoosier diet of fried Spam, hog jowls, and carrot Jell-O. She had suffered eating disorders in her youth and was still a borderline anorexic. Eventually, she became a food activist who felt that something should be done about Cyprus, where diet was a public-health scandal.

I note with some embarrassment that the careers of all my fellows emerged from similar ironies. I'd call mine a self-reactive theory of human personality, mercifully not universal. We become what we are to escape what we were.

We four raised a glass of Agios Onoufrios, the fine dry red wine of Káthikas that contrasts with Commandaria, the world's sweetest red wine, produced in the foothills of the Tróödos.

"Here's to Lord Byron and the songbirds," I proposed. "Cypriots are to songbirds as—what's his name?—Paul Ryan is to deer. Too bad. It's patriotic here to capture songbirds and pickle them."

Jasmine then reprimanded the waiter for bringing pickled songbirds. Muttering "goddam tourists" in Greek, he skulked away with four platefuls, accompanied by a dragonfly that had hovered over our table throughout the evening. I was put in mind of how difficult it would be to change native customs, an agenda regarded by some anthropologists as politically incorrect even when customs include stoning adulterers, eating people, and showing up fashionably late.

Chapter Two

THE FLYOVER

We four drove from Káthikas the following morning in our rental Bentley. As we followed the steep road toward the village of Pegeia, Gayle at the wheel, we could see the Mediterranean in its painterly deep blue, the nurturing sea that had risen eleven inches in the past decade and now threatened the sea turtle hatcheries. There stood the noble conical sphere of Yeronisos Island a couple hundred yards off Cape Drepano.

At Páphos International Airport, we boarded a Cessna Citation Mustang, a five-seater with two jet engines. This would be no joyride but a scientific expedition to see firsthand the lay of the island and collect data. The aircraft was retrofitted by Soros foundation engineers according to specs that answered to our specialties—from recording devices not unlike those in the U-2 spy plane of yore to spectrometers for divining crop, forest, floral display, and irrigation patterns; to heat sensors that judged which portions of the island were most damaged by desertification, and numerical counters that could monitor vehicles and pedestrian traffic. We had the scanning technology Lidar, which could discern ancient human artifacts and ruins as it surveyed the ground with billions of laser beams. We had sensors sensitive to cultural differences between Turkish and Greek Cypriots in dress, body type, hair style, and even facial expression, the latter based on dubious sociological data that Turks were likely to appear dour and Greeks merry.

Programmed by geeks at Rockefeller University, these cultural sensors also gauged the progress of de-resettlement, as many dispossessed Cypriot Turks moved back south and many dispossessed Cypriot Greeks moved back north. Naturally we had a computer capable of crunching terabytes in our quest for significant patterns. We could leave most of this to Agamemnon, or Agie, as we called him.

Four sets of eyes couldn't be supplanted by Agie altogether. My own set wasn't enhanced by modern technologies, since the import of literature cannot yet be accurately judged from the air. This is changing through the digital interception of all downloaded books, including this one, and soon their interpretation by digital minds sharper than our merely biological ones. I myself was on the scene to take stock of those taking stock. Whether my books and others will be forever vaporized by Clouds that judge them ideologically subversive is anybody's guess.

Wearing goggles and her seasoned Snoopy cap, which bore small resemblance to Neil Armstrong's, Gayle took command of the strategically modified Cessna while Jasmine took Valium.

"Okay folks, prepare for takeoff. This oughta be a breeze," said Gayle, "but I gotta negotiate a short runway with a heavily equipped aircraft. Big Al survived my flying and I only had a beginner's license."

The plane varoomed down the runway until a recorded voice in English with a heavy Greek accent bellowed, "Abort takeoff, abort takeoff! Fast! Now! Faster!"

Gayle threw the two small jet engines in reverse and we came to a halt within a few meters of the runway's end. "Hmmm," she said, "seems Jasmine and Darcy are gonna have to switch sides. Jasmine, you're too skinny to sit on the left, and Darcy, you're too fat to sit on the right. Has to do with placement of the gravimeter."

Jasmine took a second Valium and this time up, up and away we flew. Darcy was in a funk again. Seems he hadn't taken to the idea that as a vegetarian he could be termed *fat*—I'd guess twenty-five percent of his biomass was chips—and this from the very fellow to whom he was warming.

Gayle specialized in near vertical upswing. Within minutes we were at eight thousand feet with a view of the entire island.

Let's leave off the human comedy and turn to Great Creating Nature, whose splendid panorama stretched out in full sublimity. To the northwest we could see the coast as far as the Akámas peninsula, to the northeast the Tróödos mountains and beyond them the Pendadháktylos range. To the far east the Karpaz peninsula, below it Cape Gréko, and directly to the east the Limassol foothills. It was so much the bounty of nature that I feared myself incapable of taking it all in.

Panorama gave way to closer scrutiny as we first winged north, descending along the Páphian coast. Having had her bit of fun, Gayle settled in at about five hundred feet, slowed the craft, did a volte-face, and headed southeast along the coast. The first major site was on our left, the Pétra toú Romíou, the stately limestone formations where Aphrodite first came ashore on white foam. Then another volte-face as we flew inland over the village of Koúklia and the remains of Palaepaphos, site of Aphrodite's shrine for a millennium where, according to Herodotus, every apprentice prostitute was required to have sex with a stranger to earn her certificate.

"When we meet Melusina," I said, referring to our archeologist, "she'll tell us whether Aphrodite was a major deity or a minor whore." I was trying to entertain while Jasmine and Darcy were still in recovery. "Her cult thrives, despite Emperor Theodosius's ban on pagan rites in the fourth century." We looked down on a pile of broken columns. "Look, you can see tourists lining up at her shrine."

"But her lover promised her an oasis where we now have desert," said Gayle, looking back at her passengers. I felt she should perhaps pay more attention to where she was going. "That's why I'm here, to make Cyprus the oasis of the Mediterranean."

The enchanted island looked so parched Gayle would need to be a major deity herself to put living flesh on those bare bones, however lovely.

We continued northwest and followed the coast off Páphos, looking down to our right at Páphos Castle and the Old Customs House, then the houses of Theseus, Orpheus, and Dionysus, where the fine Roman mosaics were uncovered. Then past the Tombs of the Kings, looted by the infamous American consul Cesnola. His plunder became the first installation in the Metropolitan Museum of New York.

Gayle dipped to about two hundred feet for a flyby of the isle of Yeronisos—prearranged so that we could wave to Melusina, festooned in a white toga and standing amid Roman columns, waving back as her divers sat in two semicircles facing each other.

"Whatever their fuss is over," I said, "Melusina is known for waging love, not war. She'll resolve it."

Gayle flew the craft up the western coast over the turtle hatcheries of Cape Lára. Darcy took out his high-powered binoculars. "If anybody can save the bloody turtles and songbirds, it's me!"

Gayle looked back at us and rolled her eyes, then the plane itself just for emphasis. But Jasmine seemed impressed. "Let me be your sous chef, Darcy," she said with warmth. Darcy, having turned away from her, was addressing the bulk of his gibberish to Gayle.

Gayle headed up the Akámas peninsula, desolate, depopulated, and impassable except by jeep. Circling around the tip and heading east, we could see the baths of the love goddess, where she met with Adonis annually in the spring and where anybody who thinks it worth the risk can break a prohibition against swimming and be instantly restored to youth. Failing this, you can settle for regained virginity by swimming three times around Pétra toú Romíou. If you swim around only twice, two-thirds of virginity is regained.

Gayle announced that data collection required we now head inland toward the Tróödos mountains, encountering first Tripylos and the mouflon enclosure. Darcy's heart leapt up when he saw a small herd of the rare wild sheep. "There they are, *Ovis musimon!* Gayle, look!" he cried.

I looked down at the huge gnarled horns of the legendary beasts, whose pedigree on the island extends back before the Neolithic. They almost went extinct because they're tastier than run-of-the-mill sheep. Darcy hoped to repopulate the island with as many mouflon as humans.

"Sea turtles, songbirds, and mouflon—my Trinity! . . . Gayle, are you listening?" Gayle was unresponsive, looking down at her knuckles.

As we neared the Tróödos, with ornate Byzantine monasteries adjacent to abandoned copper mines, I peered down at the governor's residence, built by the British in 1880. I marveled at the improbabilities of life, for here Arthur Rimbaud himself had supervised a party of some fifty exploited construction workers. I looked forward to seeing the English plaque I'd already memorized— *Arthur Rimbaud, French poet and genius, despite his fame contributed with his own hands to the construction of this house, 1881.* As the great adventurer Colin Thubron points out, Rimbaud built nothing with his own hands, was not yet famous, and by 1881 had already struck out for Abyssinia.

Gayle turned around again, smiling quizzically as she took her hands off the controls and the aircraft bolted downward. "Bart, what's this infatuation you have with Rimbaud? What do you hope to find? Hundreds have already made the pilgrimage. Rimbaud is the Bob Dylan of Cyprus. Let's say you turn up his lost notebook, then what? You spend the rest of your life editing and translating? Don't get me wrong, we should follow our bliss—I do." With her right hand she reached around and pinched my left knee, hard.

"Ouch! Keep your eyes on the road, Gayle . . . Can't explain, but whenever I have insomnia I recite 'Bateau ivre' to myself—in French, naturally—that means *drunken boat.* When I get through the twenty-first stanza I fall asleep. Loosely translated—'I who, tremulous, heard groaning underseas . . . The rut of Behemoths and giant water-jets . . . Eternal gypsy of blue immobilities . . . I long for Europe and her ancient parapets.' It's the boat that's drunk, not the sailors! I like this transfer of consciousness to a nonhuman object, takes me out of myself, like Keats's nightingale singing of faery lands forlorn. We're looking at a faery land right now. It's just that Cyprus is no Eden."

"Bart, maybe you should be writing lyrical poems instead of novelistic memoirs or whatever," said Gayle, who, to judge by my throbbing knee, seemed to take an interest in me. For my part, she was too aggressive, hip, and all-American Waspish—someone who'd be more compatible with a brash middle-aged English zoologist like Darcy than an older melancholic scribbler from Ottawa.

"I *read* poetry, don't write the stuff. I'm no Lawrence Durrell."

Gayle abruptly veered northeast. "He's next on our list. We'll fly up to Kyrenia and get a bead on his house near Béllapais Abbey. Hang on!"

As we flew over ancient Mórfou, where the corpse of St. Mamas leaks out a liquid that cures earaches, the Pendadháktylos range, topped with Lusignanian castles, came into view. This range has narrow peaks instead of the rounded summits of the Tróödos. To the south we could see the vast flat Mesaoría plain that unites the two mountain ranges and provides the island with much of its grain—known as a dull "breadbasket" that tourists avoid.

The plane began bobbing up and down on turbulent updrafts. Jasmine announced she was going to be sick—this in an aircraft equipped with cyanide pills but no air-sickness bags.

"Just open the emergency door and let loose," instructed Gayle. Jasmine tossed her cookies onto the ancient city of Lápithos, known for casinos and gays.

"Sorry about that," she gasped. "Hope I didn't hit anybody in the LGBTQ community."

We reached Kyrenia, and I peered down at the medieval harbor and Kyrenia Castle with its Venetian walls, and the Dome Hotel, immortalized in *Bitter Lemons*, where Durrell describes the geriatric British holdovers emerging from their bedrooms to the waterfront by means of "crutches, trusses, trolleys, slings, and breeches-buoys," awaiting afternoon high teas and oblivious to the rich culture of the native inhabitants.

Our cultural monitor was now clicking furiously. It had accelerated ever since we began flying over the old Turkish occupation zone. I felt my heart accelerate as we approached the steep incline in Béllapais where Durrell purchased his large house on the cheap for three hundred pounds back in 1953. First we flew over the thirteenth-century Gothic abbey that took a hard hit from the Turks in 1570 but had already gone into a decline brought on by Genoese friars. They accepted as novices only those male offspring of their own concubines. This practice has its counterpart in today's college admissions committees that privilege legacy applicants.

We saw the medieval refectory used by the Brits in the late eighteen hundreds as an indoor shooting range. Then we gazed down at the roof and balcony of Lawrence Durrell's house, high in the village where Durrell wrote *Justine*, far from the din of modern Alexandria. The garden of lemon trees, pomegranates, mulberries, and a tall walnut tree was fully visible. Durrell's brother Gerald had encaged many smelly native beasts during visits here.

"We must return!" exclaimed Darcy. "Lawrence is your hero and Gerald is mine. Are you with us, Gayle?" She was silent.

"Oddly enough, for two ambitious brothers, they got along," I said.

We could see the balcony that offered views of Béllapais Abbey and Kyrenia Castle. I envied Lawrence Durrell his good luck, for not only was the late nineteenth-century house a steal, it also offered him an entrée into Turkish Cypriot culture, a wealth of endearing anecdotes, a superb view. It was a brave new world opening up, giving him good material and a future. I felt an affinity because, like him and Colin Thubron, I knew the languages and was a quick study of diverse cultures. But I lacked their quantum of energy, was easily dejected, and never felt what Wordsworth had the gall to say of himself, that he was a "chosen son." My Cyprus experiment was a fervent self-help remedy—but would it work?

Gayle looked around and caught me in a funk. "Why are you frowning when you oughta be ecstatic?"

Just then came the warning at one hundred decibels, "Your aircraft is running out of fuel! Land now! Now!"

"Prepare for an emergency landing at Nicosia," said Gayle matter-of-factly. "Sorry about that."

Jasmine took her third Valium and I regretted being an atheist as one of the engines gave out and the other spluttered. Gayle's Turkish was deficient, so I dealt with the air-traffic controllers at Ercan airport as she brought the plane down, gliding silently except for Jasmine's screams when the second engine shut down.

"Time for lunch," said Gayle. "We tank up along with the plane. Should've checked the fuel gauge before we took off. It's like rental cars. Hertz sometimes sends you off with half a tank. Same with the Soros, but they mean well."

"I'm bloody hungry," said Darcy. "And Jasmine, you need food, all skin and bones. Gayle, does this airport have a two-star restaurant?"

"Sorry, this airport doesn't have a vending machine," she replied, "but our resident nutritionist packed a picnic. Jasmine, show him your spread. Let's deplane and have it near the tarmac—under that banana tree."

Jasmine seemed eager to please Darcy, who seemed eager to please Gayle, who seemed eager to please me. All this I gauged by who offered food to whom as we sat cross-legged and dipped into the picnic basket. With Darcy in mind, Jasmine had fashioned a vegetarian menu, supplemented by Káthikas red and zivanía, which I felt Gayle should drink somewhat less of. But Darcy kept filling her amphora. "Gayle, have another on me, ha!"

We had *rókka*, *kolokássia*, hummus, tahini, and *glystrida*. Jasmine insisted that Darcy eat more and then more. She pressed ripe black Cypriot olives to his lips while, ignoring her, he chewed and talked doggedly to Gayle. After a drunken nap in which Jasmine positioned her head on the belly of Darcy who positioned his head on the belly of Gayle who positioned her head on the belly of me— and I positioned my head on an obliging agama lizard Darcy befriended—we reboarded the Cessna and flew southeast in the direction of Famagusta and Salamis.

These two cities give rise to as much enchantment as the Baths of Aphrodite—odd, given that Famagusta is the site of the most infamous massacre in the history of Cyprus, and Salamis is where all Gentiles were slaughtered during the Jewish revolt of AD 116, not the proudest episode in the history of Judaism. From the air we could see the ancient amphitheater, colonnade, and palaestra, and the nearby latrine with a seating capacity of forty-four—elimination being, as the *Rough Guide to Cyprus* tells us, for the Romans, a social occasion. I was less interested in these antiquities than in the intrigue associated with Famagusta, especially its literary association with *Othello*, and I wished to return by land to case out Othello's citadel, next to the Sea Gate.

A driving force in my narrative, as in Shakespeare's play, is jealousy. Though you are hardly reading tragic drama, be assured the yellow bile will play its usual mischief.

Soon we encountered the nearly nude bathers of Nissi Beach off Ayia Napa, where Gayle flew in for a closer look. We waved at them and they at us. We took out our binoculars to focus on Scandinavian youth, who in their fleshly display upstaged the Venetian Monastery of Agia Napa, "The Holy Virgin of the Forest," where an eighth-century icon of the Virgin was sniffed out one day by a hunter's dog. Cyprus has a mingling of the sacred and profane to rival Keats's great narrative, *The Eve of St. Agnes*.

Then it was time to head back to Páphos. We flew over Larnaca, where many of us would be presenting our cutting-edge discoveries at international conferences. We paid our respects to the Hala Sultan Tekke mosque, third most holy site in all of Islam, where we saw no pilgrims and only a few proprietary feral cats. Agie did a quick digital count of the flamingoes gathered at the Great Salt Lake—31,415 of them. We flew over Khoirokoitia, one of the oldest Neolithic settlements on the island, where humans were buried under large boulders so they can't haunt the living. We soared past Limassol, famous for its early September wine festival and little else besides money laundering, and on to ancient Kourion, unrivaled Roman site where Gayle almost got us entangled with hang gliders. Then back to Páphos, where we deplaned, thinking we'd had enough of Cyprus for one day. Even the dragonfly that shared our cabin during the flyover looked beat.

This was the first of many flights Gayle would be taking in a full mapping of the island on many levels—geologic, meteorological, agricultural, and cultural. Assume that all these flights involved some risk, because Gayle seemed inclined to tempt fate at every turn.

Chapter Three

ENHANCING MIRROR NEURONS

In that first flight, except for its airport, we circumnavigated Nicosia, until recently a divided city. The wall dividing the north and south enclaves was now converted into an elevated walkway modeled on Manhattan's High Line. The strategic reunification came about when younger left-leaning Cypriots of both North and South, possessed of social-media skills beyond those deployed in the Arab Spring, organized a strike of all public-sector workers, including sanitation engineers. The stench, encouraged by the unrelenting sun, was so great that their elders were forced either to resolve long-standing political differences or to suffocate. But not all Cypriots could alter deeply embedded aversions overnight. A few Turkish Cypriots and a few Greek Cypriots still wished one another not so much well as dead.

This was the greatest single challenge for the think tank, and I looked to our neurologist, Albert Vygotsky, renowned for his early work on mirror neurons—those nerve cells that fire up when people see others' actions and emotions—to set up an experiment that would have import not only for Cyprus but for any society that might have some latent preference for festive communal dining over throat-cutting, turning airplanes into explosive missiles, waterboarding, prayer breakfasts, drone strikes, anthrax in the water supply, and shoulder-carried nukes.

The leading authorities in mirror-neuron research—V. S. Ramachandran, Giacomo Rizzolatti, Christian Keysers, V. Gazzola, S. D. Preston, and F. de Waal spring to mind, yes?—cite Vygotsky as the pioneer in the field. He intended to extend his work on rodents to humans, with practical import for world peace if successful. He was thought to be in the running for the Nobel Prize in Medicine but maybe the Peace Prize as well. Take note, Linus Pauling. When I emailed him to suggest that Greek and Turkish Cypriots might better serve as human subjects than embittered married couples on the Upper East Side, he replied, *Why did I not think of this? I'll sign on. Do not expect a percentage of my prize money. Sincerely yours, Dr. Albert Vygotsky, Distinguished University Professor.*

These days, the basic biochemistry of mirror neurons is taught in middle school biology. I assume you know this much. Albert had been fabricating a biopsychotropic agent that would enhance synaptic connectivity among mirror neurons much the way that antidepressant drugs enhance serotonin. At least in theory, those taking Albert's concoction would so empathize with their blood enemies that they would send a bottle of champagne to their table and offer to pay off their mortgages. Such activity had been observed among rats previously tribal and aggressive. It remained to set up an experiment with humans. One group would be administered the drug, patented by Albert as Empathomax, and those in a control group would receive a placebo. Albert would be in the dark as to which group was which, this being a double-blind experiment.

The Food and Drug Administration quickly approved the ethics since only ethnics would be endangered. Internet pop-ups offering plentiful euros to volunteers were placed on listserves near Káthikos. Back in the States, Albert set up his protocol, appointing a disinterested committee at Rockefeller to select applicants on the basis of "degree of hatred" concerning their Greek or Turkish counterparts. The experimental design wasn't intended to select a sample group representative of the larger Cypriot population but only a subgroup in whom ethnic prejudice remained extreme.

Albert's serum would be all the more worthy of a Nobel if it could convert bullies into buddies.

Feelings about food were markers of ethnic resentment. If a Greek Cypriot wrote disparagingly of *kunefe*, a Turkish cheese pastry, he became a prime candidate. If a Turkish Cypriot wrote "to hell with *haloumi*," she advanced up the list. The e-questionnaire also encouraged negative remarks about the opposition group's personal hygiene, drinking habits, beard length, size of nose, and girth of waist. Applicants were asked what factions their ancestors sided with during the time of troubles, which, not unlike Ireland, was all the time. The committee made a selection of twenty-six Turkish Cypriots and twenty-six Greek Cypriots, evenly divided as to sex.

The Sappho Manor House, located in the nearby village Dhroúsha, was purchased by the Soros foundation. It had a kitchen large enough to be converted into a laboratory. A one-way window permitted Albert to record what was said and done during the hour-long sessions. Each pair, a male and female of the opposing ethnic group, would be left alone, whether to chat, argue, spit, or fuck. No weaponry could be taken into the room and no alcohol. This was science, not tribalism continued by other means. At the suggestion of Darcy, who had read a book by his compatriot Donald Winnicott, Albert asked me to provide some "transitional objects" to serve a communicative role, and two dictionaries—one Greek to Turkish and the other Turkish to Greek. With some perversity, as I always hoped for good material, I selected a small totemic plank figurine that predated both Jesus and Mohammed, fixings for coffee both Greek and Turkish, a famished stray cat, a bag of Iams cat food for mature cats, a bowl of figs that could pass for either Turkish or Greek, an irritating grandfather clock, a score sheet for no game in particular, a Lego set of Saint Hilarion Castle, a stuffed pink flamingo, and a bell ringer for room service.

I had never seen Albert in person, but when he showed up the day after our flyover, it was easy to see why he was taken for a potential terrorist at Athens airport. He skulked as if guilty of something and crouched as if to appear shorter and less conspicuous than his five foot ten. The ragged raincoat, out of place in parched Athens, could have concealed a suicide vest. Airport security may have had the same jittery response as I to his evasive throat-clearings and averted eyes. When I introduced myself, I felt as if I were speaking to one of Jonathan Swift's Laputans, for he limply shook my hand while holding his head at a right angle to my own. I wondered if he had any mirror neurons of his own. He did have large features—black eyes deeply set, shaggy eyebrows, prominent proboscis, lips full if pallid, and deep furrows, maybe from a lifetime of being a worrywart. It was a face worthy of the stage but he seemed hard at work not to let it serve as an expressive instrument, sucking it inward, as it were.

Unlike the other fellows, Albert said little about himself over the next few weeks. I'll tell you what I know, summarized from a lengthy entry on Wikipedia and gossipy internet sites. Born in 1965, Albert Vygotsky was descended from Ashkenazi Jews who escaped from Belarus in advance of the Nazi invasion of Lithuania in 1941 and, after a journey that included Japan and China, ended up in Brooklyn. Albert's grandparents spoke Yiddish, his parents spoke Yiddish, Hebrew, and English, and he became adept in all three.

Escaping the Nazis is hardly synonymous with escaping anti-Semitism, and Albert got a good dose in his rough-and-tumble Bensonhurst neighborhood, where he was taunted as an "oven-dodger" and told, "You were there, weren't you, *weren't you?*" as in *when they crucified my Lord.* At the prestigious Bronx High School of Science, where he graduated valedictorian and gained admission to Caltech, he was mysteriously not elected by the faculty to the National Honor Society. A few times he tried to date shiksas but was told by their parents that he should stick with his own kind. Perhaps this fostered an inveterate paranoia and inability to look others in the eye, an obliquity in his dealings with others that made Rockefeller University all the more appealing. It was easier for him to peer into a cage of rats than into a classroom of humans, and Rockefeller did not ask that its faculty teach.

We all gave lots of rope to the Nobelist-to-be and found that after he had some zivanía taken, he became rather talkative and almost sociable. That evening at the taverna, our numbers having swelled to five, he shared something of how he produced his promising serum.

"Only time I failed to get a grant from the NIH or NSF was when I applied for work on mirror neurons in the early nineties. They thought I was nuts."

"Well, *are* you?" asked Gayle. She posed this question for the rest of us.

"I'll get the last laugh in Stockholm," said Albert. "Just wait."

"So how'd you manage your research with no grant?" I asked.

"Easy. I got it right the first time. Didn't need to set up control groups or deal with negative results. These don't make news unless you're refuting Einstein."

"What were your positive results?" asked Jasmine.

"Coming to that . . . *zei shtil.*" He turned at a right angle to us all. "All I needed were two rats and one cage. I injected the rats with my serum and attached electrodes to their obtuse craniums. They glowed with empathy. Downright embarrassing. The younger rat offered his seat to the decrepit rat eighty-five consecutive times with no positive reinforcement, no rat matzah. It was virtue for virtue's sake, not that stimulus-response crap."

"Seat, what seat?" asked Darcy.

"I bought a rat-sized seat—found one at a dollhouse emporium on lower Fifth Ave. The whole experiment cost twenty-three dollars. The electrodes were discards from a garage in Brooklyn. The serum was free, derived from Passover leftovers, can't give you the formula."

"This is what the French theorists call *bricolage,*" I put in, hoping to elevate our discourse. "You make do with what you find on the ground."

"Or in the back of the fridge," said Jasmine. "I can put together leftovers and serve a meal worthy of the Romanoffs. Just wait for my vegetarian goulash, Darcy." Darcy was silent.

The following morning the experimental subjects began reporting to Sappho Manor House for the first of their one-hour sessions, twice a week. They were welcomed by Albert with all the warmth of a county magistrate handling parking violations. I don't have space to describe all twenty-six couples so will focus throughout this history on the single true standout.

Have I mentioned that I'm a lapsed Catholic? I have an ambiguous attitude toward religion, seeing it as answering the desperate needs of the human psyche and being the source of many of our greatest artistic works but responsible also for more senseless deaths per square mile on this planet than any other toxin except the Black Death.

This particular couple represented a holy war in miniature—Armide Asani, a Turkish Cypriot and worshipper of Mohammed, and Renaud Remis, an Eastern Orthodox Greek Cypriot and worshipper of Jesus Christ. I watched as Albert administered the serum with all the subtlety of a Spanish inquisitor, brandishing a large needle before their eyes with a smirk.

When first left alone in the observation room, the two snarled and hissed on director's chairs from opposing corners. In part the nonverbal aggression was the result of not sharing a language. Lack of knives or handguns left open the threats of fists, fingernails, and teeth. But Armide and Renaud settled down on their director's chairs and began toying with the transitional objects.

Armide was a petite woman of twenty-one and possibly a rare beauty but difficult to tell under the lime-green niqab that covered her face except for the eyes, themselves obscured by sunglasses with lime-green frames. She was atypical of most modern Turkish Cypriot women, who decline to wear niqabs, burqas, and hijabs, favoring Western European dress. Renaud had a darkish complexion, a three-day growth, the breath of someone who drinks strong coffee and smokes cigarettes all morning before taking any food, and the beginnings of a paunch at twenty-two from sitting around drinking ouzo late afternoons. He dressed in faded denims and a sagging T-shirt, but was tall and otherwise fit. I cannot judge whether he was handsome. He was atypical of younger Greek Cypriots in his great hostility toward Turkish Cypriots and the Muslim world in general, for reasons I could never ascertain.

Armide stood up and approached the famished cat. "What's your name, cat?" she asked in Turkish.

Renaud mistook her as asking the cat why she was so fucking skinny. "Obviously this cat needs some food, bitch," he observed in Greek.

Each ran for a dictionary, Renaud to confirm the Turkish for *fucking*, and Armide to confirm the Greek for *bitch*. Armide was the first to have her hunch confirmed, so she picked up the stuffed flamingo in a threatening way and Renaud the plank figurine.

"In the name of Mohammed the Prophet I shall blind your infidel eyes with this bird's beak!" she cried in Cypriot Turkish.

"In the name of Jesus the Pantocrator I shall plunge this plank into your belly until you faint at the sight of your own guts!" he replied in Cypriot Greek.

At this point Albert called off the session, I acting as interpreter and regretting that I'd not edited out some of those transitional objects. "Participants, homicide is against the ground rules. If slay, no pay."

They backed off and, with tongue display, sat back down on the director's chairs.

Albert told me this first session had gone well in the main, so he figured they weren't receiving the placebo. After all, each had endeavored to learn the other's tongue in some measure, and each had expressed a depth of feeling toward the other that could perhaps be modified in kind.

Both picked up the promised euros and were on their separate ways as if nothing had happened.

Chapter Four

THE ARRIVAL OF MELUSINA

I had arranged for our group to stay in two domiciles by boy-girl criteria. Darcy, our zoologist, Gayle, our meteorologist, and I moved into the Anogia tóu Mikhali, which had a walled-in courtyard and steep stone staircase where many have surely broken necks over the centuries. Albert, our neurologist, Jasmine, our nutritionist, and Melusina, our archeologist, were in the Chelidonia, a stone house dating to the sixteenth century. I figured this distribution would create productive subgroups within the think tank. No false prophet here, but shouldn't I have foreseen some all-too-human entanglements?

Melusina Frei had taken over excavations on the island of Yeronisos, a few miles north of Páphos. This was the site of earlier expeditions by NYU-sponsored students who finally gave up after not finding a single intact artifact despite two decades of digging in the hot sun. The work also interfered with their sexting. Melusina reconceived the search as underwater archeology and was said to be closing in on a colossal sculpture of Aphrodite by the fabled Pygmalion himself. Legend has it that Aphrodite emerged from the sea on a giant oyster shell near Pétra toú Romíou just down the road from Páphos. It made sense that Pygmalion would carve a sculpture of the goddess near her hometown.

Melusina arrived with flair, her long blonde hair and welkin eyes set off by a purple silk scarf, chauffeured in a vintage oyster-pink Rolls Royce convertible with top down, driven by an unusually buoyant Turkish fisherman working off-hours for Poseidon Taxi Service. I figured the Turks had pilfered the costly Rolls from the Brits at some point. Melusina had left her archeological equipment back at the Yeronisos site but had five large brocade carpetbags. Why she needed all this stuff was a puzzle, for she was wearing virtually nothing beyond her scarf, a cadmium-red thong bikini, and mukluks. She thanked the cabbie in Turkish, tipping him lavishly, punched his right shoulder, and sent him on his way. Clearly he would have preferred to stay.

Except for Albert, who had more important matters to tend to, we were all outside the Chelidonia to welcome her.

"You are Bart Beasley," she said, extending a warm moist hand and nearly crushing my metacarpals. "I am loving your work, especially *In Search of the Fabled Cities of Lost Icelandia*."

"That's close, it's *In Search of the Lost Cities of Fabled Icelandia*. Flattered you read it."

"*Ja*, a brilliant fabrication. You had no authentic archeological evidence to be backing it up."

"It's called a *memoir*—the most dishonest subgenre in the house of literature, offering the greatest incentives to lie."

Melusina laughed. "Did you truly go on this quest?"

"Yes, but on an easy chair in Reykjavik, reading travelogues by real naturalists and adventurers, mostly nineteenth-century. I'd take the hotel elevator downstairs for dinner and mix with the natives. I speak Icelandic now. That must count for something."

I admit to a habit of self-deprecation so as to waylay easy assaults. With Melusina I wasn't under siege—it was clear she liked me—but proprietary Gayle rescued me anyway.

"Bart gives us truth his own way, analogous truth. He's what you call a *writer*."

"And you are Gayle Drake-Larkin. Delighted! Your reputation for daring is going before you. I have watched the viral YouTube of a figure-of-eight you have carried off beneath the Golden Gate Bridge. That took cojones."

"I do those stunts just for kicks. The real daring, *madam*, will be what I do about this island's desertification." Gayle had a self-confidence that rivaled North American shamans who take control of the weather.

"Madam? *Meine Liebste*, I'm older but not all that much. Call me Melusina. You must know I have turned to underwater archeology my Aphrodite to find. The same global warming that is melting glaciers is giving me more water to work under." She laughed at her own little joke.

"Fine for you, blinking bad for the sea turtles," put in Darcy, humorless when it came to anything threatening animals.

"Ah, and you are Darcy Peatman, the famed zoologist. Has anybody said you're a dead ringer for Stewart Granger, your garb that is? I am loving the way you refute Stephen Jay Gould and Richard Dawkins in *My Inner Animal*."

"*The Animal Within*, but close enough. That's my only theoretical book. The others are anecdotal accounts of animals I've known, like Gerald Durrell's *jeux d'ésprit*."

"I am loving Gerald Durrell!" exclaimed Melusina.

Gayle was clearly annoyed. I watched her eye the scant apparel warily, a contrast to the way people dress in Oregon—sexless raingear from L.L.Bean.

"And you are Jasmine Ivory, the eminent nutritionist!" exclaimed Melusina. The two were a study in contrasts, Jasmine's African-American hue all the darker next to Melusina's Teutonic pallor. I couldn't help but note the contrast between the German's voluptuous body parts, barely contained by the bikini, and the American's Giacometti-like minimalism disguised with loose denims and a baggy green T-shirt reading "Chickpeas oui, chips non."

"Yes, I'm a nutritionist and can't help with your archeological projects. Ancient statuary doesn't eat."

"My Aphrodite is ravenous! Hasn't eaten for millennia. By the way, I have scuttled the divers' strike. And thank you but no, I am having nothing in common with Hitler."

"Who was saying?" I interjected.

Melusina seemed at a momentary loss for words as she adjusted her thong. Yes, she was defensive about Hitler and I already knew why. Her maternal grandfather had been a member of the Ahnenerbe, the Nazi archeological think tank that tried to prove that Germans once ruled the planet. He had journeyed to Iceland to discover the site of Thule, where the Aryan race had supposedly been hatched, and also found evidence, to the satisfaction of his chum Himmler, that Poland had always been German. In their many slaughters the Germans were simply reclaiming what had always been theirs, a logic that extended to all nooks and crannies.

It was easy to conclude that Melusina's career was compensation for being saddled with such a grandfather. But inherited guilt didn't explain her bountiful good nature, self-confidence, and polyamory—more about that later.

"How did you persuade your divers to get back to work?" I asked.

"You are wanting the whole story, *Liebling*? It is beginning with a Scrabble challenge. Every evening after a long day in the drink my divers across a long table at the West End Restaurant were meeting for a Scrabble smackdown. Seven Greek Cypriots versus seven Turkish Cypriots. Sorry to say, they had imagined the game their English would improve. In Scrabble it is being better not to know what the words mean! Each side had won five matches and the eleventh the tournament would decide. I figured this had been an advance over human wave invasions."

"That's gotta be an understatement, Miss Frei," growled Gayle.

"If you are saying so, Miss Drake-Larkin. But trouble was on its way. Late in the game the Greeks have played the word *whankers* with an *h*, and the Turks have challenged it. To me as adjudicator they turned. *Jawohl*, only *wankers* without an *h* is a word according to *The Official Scrabble Players Dictionary*, that's the *OSPD*. But the Greeks have said *whankers* with an *h* would surely be found in the Official Tournament and Club Word List, that is being the *OTCWL*, of course. 'Prove that it is not!' Greek diver Takis Kayalis is demanding."

"I'm all for the Greeks!" exclaimed Darcy. "Not perfect, but they rescue more animals."

"*Danke schön*, Darcy. Only problem was that mere amateurs cannot legally the *OTCWL* access. So the Turks were not proving a negative and the Greeks were not proving a positive. It was a *Pattsituation*—you know, stalemate. They were refusing to work with each other and were staging a sit-down faceoff the next morning on Yeronisos. That's when you have flown over."

"I'm sympathetic to both sides," said Gayle. "Big Al and I tried to prove a positive-negative—that this planet is melting. The Republicans laughed."

"But this has been more complicated than global warming," continued Melusina. "Listen close. The *h* in *whankers* had a score of four but the *w*—also a four—placed on a triple-word score, as was the *s*. And the *k*—a five—on a double-letter score. The total initial tally of twenty-three multiplied twice by three, two hundred and seven points, plus the fifty the Greeks would be receiving for all their tiles using up—an astonishing two hundred and fifty-seven points. Worse, the Turks would be needing to *subtract* whatever tiles they were having from their own score. Injury was to insult added, as you say. *Wankers* with no *h* would the Greeks only fifty-seven points have given, *nicht genug* to conquer the six hundred and sixty-six points the Turks were accumulating. For my divers as much hung on this *h* as a presidential decision to be pressing the button."

"You must have come up with a diplomatic ploy of some sort," I observed.

"*Ja*, I was pondering what my divers might share and have come up with love of fame and fortune. If they were agreeing to call it a draw, I would be giving each of them special recognition at the official Aphrodite unveiling. The YouTube goes viral. With their new fame, they could be demanding a higher minimum wage for sea divers, whether Greek or Turkish. They have held a powwow, much unseemly sign language. Finally, Takis Kayalis has stood up from his semicircle and is announcing that both sides were my offer accepting. I right away have texted the Ministry of Finance to be raising their minimum wage and have got a thumbs-up emoji. My divers applauded, embraced, and kissed one another, have pulled foodstuffs out of their pockets for sharing with their enemies, and their diver's suits have put back on."

"This is encouraging," said Jasmine. "People who share food rarely off each other."

"Today they are being back at work in their diving gear pulling ancient rubble away from the site where the Aphrodite of Pygmalion is awaiting me . . . By the way, where is Albert Vygotsky, the legendary neurologist?"

I was nonplussed by Albert's lack of a sense of occasion. "Oh, he was performing a delicate mixture of mirror neurons with, er, various cortical stimulants. I'll see if he's finished."

I entered the Chelidonia where I found Albert upstairs looking anxiously at his cell phone and chewing a cuticle. "Albert, Melusina has arrived and would like to meet you. We're all outside."

"I would prefer not to."

"But why? She is really something."

"Just tell her to come up. We must settle the matter of who sleeps where. As you know, she wants the room with a view, but I shall not budge. She can stay downstairs with Jasmine and the kitchen."

Another negotiation for Melusina. I felt Albert might prove more intransigent than the divers. From the shuttered second-floor window, I waved them up, and for the first time all members of the Cyprus Think Tank were in a single space. I opened the zivanía and proposed a toast to Melusina and success in our shared mission of fixing the tortured island.

"So you are Albert Vygotsky, illustrious discoverer of mirror neurons and a likely Nobelist! Is anybody ever saying that you're a dead ringer for Harvey Fierstein?"

"No, nudnik, but *he* takes lots of ribbing." I assumed that Albert outdid himself with this fast comeback but I underestimated him. "Now Miss Frei, I empathize with your wish to expropriate the room with a view—I feel it so much myself that I shall never give it up. Downstairs, with Miss Ivory, you'll have a good view of our neighbor's outhouse."

Melusina laughed. "So you are being quite the bosser. Everybody, let us be lugging his junk downstairs. *Miss* Frei, *Miss* Ivory indeed!" Jasmine didn't raise a fuss of her own, but she would now need to move upstairs to avoid sharing sleeping quarters with Albert.

Diplomatic intervention runs in my family. "Albert, downstairs you'll be closer to the front door in the event of an earthquake, and if you yield to the archeologist she'll owe you one—right, Melusina?"

"*Jawohl,* like the fucking time of day. Here, Bart, take this carpetbag."

We were interrupted by a dragonfly that alighted on Albert's nose. "*Mein gott!*" He tried to smush it but it decamped vertically. When he gave chase, Darcy restrained him.

"That's a black-tailed skimmer, *Orthetrum cancellatum,* so named by Linnaeus in 1758. Cyprus has thirty-seven species of dragonflies and damselflies, all endangered by desertification. So lay off!"

"How do you know so much about dragonflies?" asked Jasmine.

"Oh, just happen to be the world authority. Any zoologist worth his porridge is also an entomologist. I've clocked hours in wetlands the world over, made observations of dragonflies as a hobby. Ended up the grandmaster, what can I tell you?"

"But Cyprus is hardly a wetland," noted Gayle.

"It's had enough standing pools to sustain those thirty-seven species. There are three thousand and twelve throughout the world.

Let us now praise dragonflies. They eat midges and mosquitoes. Hard for a midge to escape a dragonfly. Its eyes have twenty-four thousand ommatidia—that's segments for you know-nothings. They eat their prey head first. Ha! The Swedes believe the devil uses dragonflies to weigh our souls, and southerners in your U.S. of A., Gayle my lovely, believe they follow snakes around to repair tears in their skins. That much is bollocks."

Clearly the display of bug erudition fired up Jasmine's interest in Darcy all the more, and even Gayle seemed impressed.

But it was time to return to business. We all hopped to, yielding to Melusina while Albert watched wide-eyed.

"Come on," said Melusina to Albert, weighing a challenge to her powers. "We three are having lots to talk about—your neurons, my Aphrodite, Jasmine's foodstuffs. After a day's work we have heart-to-hearts and playful pillow fights." She gave his right cheek a tweak.

"Miss Frei, are there no boundaries?"

"Boundaries? That's what it is being all about. Aphrodite's great mission is to bring them down."

"Right you are," said Darcy. "It's worth a bloody try. Come on, everybody, let's drink to universal harmony. In a few days we visit the sea turtles. But talk about boundaries, those poor critters *need* them!"

— Chapter Five —

SAVING THE TURTLES

The night of May fifteenth Darcy led an expedition to Cape Lára, a few miles north of Yeronisos, to witness the first week of female loggerhead sea turtles arrive to lay eggs at the site of their birth twenty years earlier. Gayle, Jasmine, Melusina, and I shared the adventure, with Gayle once again at the wheel, this time a Land Rover. Albert cared not a jot for sea turtles and preferred not to come along. When we reached the beach, Darcy told Gayle to drive slowly on the sand without headlights, unnecessary because of the full moon and likely to confuse the turtles.

"The biggest threat to these noble beasts was the goddam Bishop of Páphos," he said. "Back in 1989—that's before I was on the scene—he sent lorries to load up sand for his bloody golf course. Then he tried to build a luxury hotel so sunbathers could park their butts on the very sands that belonged to the turtles. He put a curse on the environmentalists but they prevailed—got Cape Lára declared a national park and the good bishop was convicted of mail fraud and pederasty. Ha!"

"All right already," said Gayle. "You haven't done much the past few weeks except yammer on about the sea turtles and the time you've spent rescuing them. But I agree—death to the archbishop!"

Darcy looked deflated.

We silently took in Cape Lára, its sandy crescent beach luminescent in the moonlight. With climate change, the instinctive clock of the turtles had moved forward two weeks, and mid-May at nearly full moon was the appointed time of their first arrival. Every two weeks until early August they would lumber ashore, digging holes in the sand with hind flippers and laying about one hundred eggs each, then covering them so predators could not guess their whereabouts. After seven weeks the hatchlings would emerge at night, catch the reflection of the moon in the water, and head for the sea. Few make it, what with seagulls, foxes, and human-sourced light that sends them the wrong way. Only one in a thousand makes it to maturity.

When we needed to abandon the Rover and walk, Darcy had us carry large loads of mesh for protecting egg sites. Sure enough, at midnight under a nearly full moon, we witnessed a phalanx of large females making their way up the beach. They moved clumsily through the sand, their carapaces lit up in the moonlight, their primal memories taking them to the very spots where they had themselves emerged as hatchlings. What does Proust have over a primal memory that dictates the cycles of life, not merely the rich associational recall of connoisseurs of consciousness? These turtles have a memory that leads them to futurity and their survival as a species.

"Blimey!" exclaimed Darcy. "I'd like to be one for just a few minutes and then remember what it feels like to be a turtle."

"It can't feel very good," said Jasmine, "carrying all those eggs . . . like they've eaten too much. Give me a hand, Darcy. The mesh is heavy. Help me up this dune, dude."

Darcy seemed reluctant but extended a hand to Jasmine. When we reached the top of the dune, she didn't relinquish the hand. Gayle then said to me, "Hey, give me a hand, Bart. This mesh is heavy!" I proffered a hand, which she squeezed hard, and she too didn't let go. This left only Melusina not holding hands with somebody or other. I looked at her sheepishly as if to say, "I don't really wish to be holding hands with Gayle." The moonlight was strong enough that I could read Darcy's countenance. He clearly would rather have been holding hands with Gayle than Jasmine. I looked at him sheepishly too as if to say that this wasn't my idea. Melusina registered everything, laughed, and said, "Unfair when the seeker of Aphrodite out of the loop is getting left!"

But I could see that Melusina looked with real envy at Darcy and his good fortune in having Jasmine hold his hand. This was the first hint I registered of a same-sex itch among the fellows.

This is a think tank and not a kids' church camp where hand-holding opportunities present during prayer circles beneath the umbrella of piety. Here the cause was the salvation of turtles, not souls. We'd be pitching in on Darcy's trinity of turtles, songbirds, and mouflon, as well as other worthy causes, and I wondered if all might prove merely the occasion for hand-holding, to what outcomes I could only imagine.

Jasmine and Gayle, made self-conscious by Melusina's lament, let go of Darcy and me so we could focus on these five-hundred-pound turtles. We encircled one who had found the right spot for her eggs.

Darcy said, "This turtle—meet Priscilla—is about to lay eggs exactly where she hatched in 2004." He rubbed his nose on her proboscis sympathetically. "They'll be washed over at high tide and sucked out to sea—damned global warming. Bloody captains of industry, bloody politicians!" He turned back to us. "Let's try to push her and the others higher up the beach."

"Al Gore and I did what we could," said Gayle. "It's just that it's more convenient to let the next generation of sea turtles be damned."

"Drowned," said Darcy. "They need to breathe like the rest of us."

He pressed an ear to the sand and monitored the sound of nearby turtles sloshing up the beach. "Dozens are coming! Let's start with Priscilla. Come on, help give her a shove."

Priscilla didn't appreciate our attentions, snapping at us as if to say bugger off, and went ahead digging with hind flippers. Have you ever tried to budge a five-hundred-pound sea turtle up the beach? Don't. Even if we succeeded, who could say she wouldn't descend once again?

We all pitched in to move Priscilla. Darcy spoke to her in earnest about the hazards of global warming and why a higher nesting site made good sense. Seemingly convinced, she allowed us to push her higher up. Then she began digging a more advantageously situated hole. We went back for Tara, with whom Darcy was again somehow already acquainted, and gave her a push some thirty yards up the beach from her ancestral hatch site. Then Tracy, Myrtle, Phyllis, then Beulah. This was tough. I could see that at least one hundred loggerheads remained down the beach.

It was then that I registered a curious suspension of the natural order. Though we were at low tide and could expect the sea to begin swelling, it was rapidly receding. My companions were so focused on turtles that they didn't hear the low roar in the distance. I looked at the image of the moon in the receding water and saw a large ripple.

For the previous few hours all our electronic devices had mysteriously ceased working, so we were unaware of what most of the world already knew. A tsunami was headed our way, generated by a seventh-magnitude earthquake off the shore of Santorini, the mythical Lost Atlantis that just keeps on giving. While Darcy and Jasmine were pleading with a recalcitrant turtle named Cara, I called to them.

"Turn around! See what I see?"

"Hmmm, I see a wall of water maybe thirty feet high," said Darcy, vexed at being interrupted.

"Oh my God!" exclaimed Gayle. "And coming straight for us at ninety knots." She looked at us wide-eyed. "Let's bolt!"

We didn't have time to bolt before we were engulfed. We were lucky this tsunami was water only, no houses, cars, boats, plastic bottles, or human carnage. A storybook tsunami. We tried to ride the wave but Darcy had a better idea.

"Let's ride the turtles!"

He latched on to a carapace—Kelly's. We each found an obliging turtle and rode out the tsunami, beaching about two hundred yards from our starting point.

The wave receded but we knew enough to expect another, so we nestled down to monitor the sea with more than one hundred female loggerheads. The second wave arrived and again we rode the turtles even higher up the beach.

"Hey, this is fun!" cried Gayle. Melusina was the best swimmer, if not in the same league with the turtles transporting us to safety. She shoved me helpfully when I almost slipped off Tina, a hard-shelled loggerhead with a petulant personality.

The turtles now took stock, eyeing the sea and taking a hint from the tsunami. They all began laying eggs at this higher station. Darcy cheered. "This tsunami is brilliant!"

"But what about the other sea turtles—like the green turtles in the North?" I asked.

"Oh, sea turtles are clever," said Darcy. "They're like bees. They'll spread the word. They communicate with underwater hip-hop. And unlike humans they have a highly developed empathy—what's good for one turtle is good for all."

The turtles finished laying eggs and clambered down to the sea. We spread protective mesh over the many sites. Hatchlings could escape the mesh but predators couldn't invade, owing to the complex device patented by Darcy himself. I thought this an early triumph for the Cyprus Think Tank—the preservation of the renowned Cypriot sea turtles.

It was good fortune that the bulk of the tsunami waters in the southeast spilt into the reservoir created by the Southern Conveyor Project, where it could, after de-salinization, be dispatched to the rest of the island via its 110-kilometer water carrier. A few naked Russian gangsters sipping vodka on the beach near Páphos were unaccounted for, but otherwise there seemed to be no human toll.

It wasn't just Gaia giving us an assist with that beneficent tsunami. Darcy himself needed to talk the turtles into accepting their new venue—a not inconsiderable skill. Having saved the turtles, he could now turn to the songbirds and mouflon.

Chapter Six

RIMBAUD'S NOTEBOOK

In late 1878, four years after Arthur Rimbaud had given up composition of verse at the age of twenty, he arrived in Larnaca to become foreman of a nearby stone quarry. One motive was wanderlust—to escape bourgeois France and his despotic Catholic mother in Charleville, and yield to the pull of the East. Like any escapee, he needed money, so working a stone quarry in Cyprus made as much sense as any other job. But I've always thought there was a special lure in Cyprus. Rimbaud's poetry expresses a passion for Aphrodite, and this was her island. Here, as a pagan, he could escape what he charmingly termed the "putrid kisses" of Jesus.

Rimbaud was an unpopular foreman, alienating the underclass of sixty desperate laborers of different nationalities who slept in lean-tos and ate indigestible seaweed swilled down with low-grade zivanía. He slept with a dagger at the ready. It was good fortune that he came down with typhus and was forced to return to France. But he returned to Cyprus a few months later, parlaying scant credentials into being hired as construction foreman of the British governor's lackluster hunting lodge in the Tróödos. He wrote his family that it was a palace. My guess is that he got the job because of his gift for languages—he could speak English, Greek, and Arabic as well as his native French. But maybe it was also his mesmeric eyes, a celestial blue that could bewitch any employer, even a weary functionary procuring for an imperial power. Rimbaud had no political conscience and would later lend his hand to gunrunning in Abyssinia and even the slave trade. He was a visionary for hire, in the end valuing money more than poetry, and dying of a horrific leg cancer at thirty-seven.

Gayle volunteered to be my escort and driver in my search for Rimbaud's notebook. I wasn't happy about this because of her seeming attraction to me and my own fear of death. Nor was Darcy, who still imagined he could lasso Gayle as one might a mountain nanny goat, while he deflected the flirtation of poor Jasmine. But Gayle knew Rovers and claimed to be a whiz at mountain driving. We dived down E701 to Páphos and along the coastal B6, then flew up the scenic, vertiginous E802 to Kato Platres, averaging a terrifying sixty kilometers per hour. We checked into the Semiramis hotel, suites eight and nine. Gayle said we should cut costs and book a single suite, but I thought better.

We booked the Village Restaurant, where spawn of British expats still holed up and spent their days parked on sofas in anticipation of the ten starter platters of meze and main course sequelae.

The walls of our hotel were thin, so Gayle and I spoke from our separate Jacuzzis before heading out for dinner.

"My soul is a drunken boat," she sang as she splashed about. "Not bad, this hole. It would have cheered Rimbaud to sit in this tub and prep for meze, and maybe a few local party girls *comme dessert*?"

"Sure," I said, "but decadents don't enjoy pleasure, and Rimbaud was gay, or Verlaine made him so, or maybe it was the other way around. He didn't bathe. I'm not sure he even liked to eat. A real killjoy. Still a genius. He outstripped Shakespeare, who couldn't write anything immortal until he was nearing thirty."

"Do you really think we'll find that notebook?"

"I hope so . . ."

"Where did Rimbaud live before he ran off?"

"His biographers have little to say on his two stays in Cyprus. He lived in a wooden barrack during the second with a British engineer who knew something about construction. Rimbaud did not. He wrote his mother asking her to send *Le Livre de Poche de Charpentier*—that's *Carpentry for Dummies*. After he fled the construction site he stayed for just a few days at the Troödhitissa monastery. We'll get there by mountain bike—sorry, no Rover. You go in drag because they don't admit women. And only Greek Orthodox, so we'll cross palms."

Over dinner I sounded my companion out, feeling we should have no misunderstandings. "Not to be presumptuous but I sense your interest in me, Gayle. Let's face it, I'm old, you're young. I'm a writer. That means I'm a narcissist and can't fall in love. It's a failing, but I've never been in love. Never. Sometimes I'm infatuated but it's always with exotic, inappropriate women. It's only fantasy—you know, writing by other means. You've got spunk, you're compelling. I like your Snoopy cap, but you're not exotic, even to a Canadian. Nothing more American than Portland, Oregon, and working for Al Gore. Let's keep a lid on things, okay? It's you, not me . . . er, other way around." Couldn't believe I'd just said any of this.

"*Not exotic?* . . . Get lost! There's nobody like me. I'm *sui generis*—see, I know my Latin. Let me have my likings, Bart. You know what I like? Older men who have trouble getting it up. From my end of things, that means no pressure. Exactly what you want in a girl, right?"

She was on the mark. My history of romantic encounters had been lamentable and yes, I preferred filling notepads to privates. My best times—and here I join legions of my generation—were make-out back seat trysts in the late seventies.

"An Italian on a Fulbright got the idea we should get married and I was too polite to say no. I went from premarital bliss to marital agony to what should have been postmarital inoculation, all by twenty-three. You're better off with, well, Darcy. He's older, if not old, and probably can't get it up, but who am I to say? And you share an interest in the future of this planet. I know he, er, likes you."

"I just don't feel it for Darcy, and anyway Jasmine wants to get her mitts on him. She even told me to convince Darcy I'm not interested so she can make a move. I don't wanna cross a Black nutritionist, not PC. I keep telling Darcy, go jump in the Thames. He's better at animal communication and just doesn't get it. Jasmine has no reason to be jealous, but I'm afraid she is."

"Pretty obvious Melusina has a liking for Jasmine—luminous white on radiant black, like an electrical charge."

"She's bi, you know, and she and Jasmine are sharing pillows, but Jasmine is resistant 'cause she's never swung that way, and she still has this het-thing for Darcy."

This prattle continued over dinner to no particular conclusion. Don't ask for deep explanations of these sundry crushes. I can't enter the minds of the fellows except by skeptical and pesky inference. If you insist otherwise, go read a romance novel, not an honest memoir. My feeling is that human attachments are subrational at best and contingent on who is at hand. It's a supply theory of the affections. That deepest explorer of the human psyche, Shakespeare, knew this well enough. When did you last see *A Midsummer Night's Dream* or *As You Like It*? Beyond superficial hunches I'm at a loss why Jasmine would take an interest in Darcy, or how Darcy could think himself a candidate for Gayle, or why Gayle would grab at my knee, or why . . . well, there is more to come. Some evidence will emerge that not all lovers love at first sight. And I'll say more in time about the cards dealt, pinches, and caresses that funneled into the making of us fellows.

Gayle and I pecked each other's cheeks outside suite eight and bedded down separately. Next morning, after an English breakfast of slimy bacon, rubbery scrambled eggs, and a slab of limp dough the waiter called a croissant, we set out on our rental mountain bikes toward Pródhromos, an alpine settlement. There sits the

Troödhitissa monastery, some eight kilometers northwest of Platres and at twelve hundred meters the highest active monastery on the island.

As we peddled through pine forest, Gayle, leading the way, was wearing a fake moustache, a nineteenth-century bowler instead of her Snoopy into which she tucked her long tawny hair, and a sexless L.L.Bean cargo vest. A black-tailed skimmer buzzed her left ear, then attacked my nose like a kamikaze. Darcy wasn't there so I tried to whop it but missed. Gayle looked back, little concerned about where she was going, and kept up her questioning about Rimbaud. Why my interest? Why this monastery?

"Rimbaud wasn't only the greatest literary prodigy, he was the planet's most disgusting human being," I said, peddling past boulders and trying to keep up. "He was a sadomasochist obsessed with buttocks and feces, a gunrunner, a slave trader. Oh, by the way, a murderer."

"Murderer?"

"Little doubt. In Larnaca he used more explosives than needed in his quarry work because he liked violence, and it kept his workers awake. Let's stop a minute and catch our breath."

We sat back to back on a pine stump, and I dipped into my reservoir of patient explanation. "In his second stay he left his job abruptly again, claiming in a letter home that he had a disagreement with his paymaster and the British engineer. He'd seek work elsewhere. The story didn't come out until after his death that he'd thrown a stone at a worker in a rage. Killed him. Rather than confront a British constable, he ran off."

"But why this monastery?"

"Rimbaud was a conman. He understood religion and could talk his way into monasteries. They needed a clerk for the Cave of the Virgin Troödhitissa. He thought he could hide out there, so he applied for the clerkship. Spoke many languages and knew some arithmetic. These were credentials enough. He charged one drachma for entry into the sacred cave. For a few nights he slept in a monastic cell on a wooden bed. When the British agents were seeking him for questioning, he ran off. Caught a freighter to Egypt and ended up in Abyssinia as a coffee merchant."

"But how do you know he was keeping a notebook and why would he leave it behind?"

"I'm a sleuth. Rimbaud applied for the position of clerk at the cave. Didn't take a genius, I saw that he applied the same day he fled the construction site. The Brits had just taken over the island from the Ottomans and were keeping close records, just like the East India Company. Tons of records nobody ever looks at. When he saw the British authorities march up to the monastery, he ran off in such a hurry that he left all his belongings behind. The monastery held on to his junk and refused to hand anything over to the Brits because of the inviolability of sanctuary. And anyway they hated British guts and sort of liked this young Frenchman who spoke exquisite Cypriot Greek. But the Brits pried out of them that the belongings included some lice-ridden clothes, a dagger, a clay pipe, an empty flask, and . . . a magenta notebook! They couldn't read French, so they didn't bother with it. I figure they didn't much care about a dead Turkish Cypriot anyway. Magenta was Rimbaud's favorite color, so this notebook was something he valued."

Gayle sighed as she took all this in.

"The cave—let's call it a grotto—has an annex full of rotting volumes. The monks haven't bothered doing an inventory. It's all crumbling. They don't know what they have. One thing I've learned in life is that archivists never know what they have. I want to get into that annex and look for a magenta volume tucked away somewhere."

"How much is it worth?"

"Maybe twenty million dollars. Not much next to a Warhol or what trailer trash can win in a lottery . . . I'll probably have it auctioned at Christie's after I've translated it into English, Russian, Italian, Hindi, Greek, Turkish, and Icelandic."

We got back on our bikes and soon beheld the thirteenth-century monastery near where the icon of the Virgin is kept. This icon flew under its own steam from Asia Minor to Cyprus in the eighth century. Because iconoclasts were on the alert with hammers, the Virgin was guarded around the clock for centuries by malodorous hermits. No need for candles because the icon miraculously lit up the grotto on its own, but this made her all the more difficult to hide.

"So they haven't known all this time they have an artifact worth more than their Virgin?"

"Why would the monks know anything about Rimbaud? The only words they use are from the four communal liturgies, and their study is confined to the Greek Orthodox Bible and church fathers."

We got vetted at the gatehouse, where Gayle and I passed for Greek Orthodox owing to my gift for inflection. We made our way up the path to the grotto where a clerk charged us one euro each. This was an untidy venue with a pile of old books for sale in an annex. And sure enough, near the bottom was the magenta spine I was looking for. I hauled it out as if at random and acted indifferent. It was inscribed by hand on the cover. They were asking two euros. These I handed over, blocking an impulse to bargain them down a bit, and purchased a couple of dated guidebooks for two euros more to dilute any attention given the notebook. I was nervous when the clerk filled out a receipt, slowly writing "Cahier II A. Rimbaud" in mistransliterated Greek. But he was happy with his four euros. Sworn to silence within the grotto, Gayle and I crossed ourselves before the icon and kissed the lip-smudged glass that encased it. Sure enough, the icon glowed, but I suspected a twenty-five-watt bulb placed cunningly to enhance its supernaturalism.

Gayle's cargo vest had a back pocket large enough to hold the multimillion-dollar notebook as we happily rode back on our bikes to Platres.

Chapter Seven

INFERNAL ILLUMINATIONS

You may think you are reading a sequence of headlong adventures and a checklist of all troubles the Cyprus Think Tank will address. But beneath this utopian narrative of hope there lurks the dark underbelly of all idealism. Beyond all other writers, Rimbaud describes in his poetry and underscores in his pitiable life this underbelly. We ignore it at our peril, if you will permit a modest Canadian to proclaim himself the night watchman.

Prepare for a journey into the inferno as I become the first reader of Rimbaud's lost notebook and this werewolf-as-poet's visionary encounter with powers of darkness. I'd already felt an affinity with the prodigy, not his genius but our dismay with provincial life, for his Charleville was my Ottawa. I like to think we also shared an acuity of the senses and a wish, as he famously put it once in a letter, to "disorder" them. Explaining what Rimbaud meant by a "long, immense and reasoned disordering of the senses" has secured tenure for countless assistant professors of French.

Give up the life of writing? His resolve, not mine, but there was always some Bartleby the Scrivener in me. "I would prefer not to" is a useful mantra for anybody wishing to ward off all importunities of the will from within and irksome demands from without. We've heard Albert deploy it.

Shortly after discovering the notebook, I translated passages that seemed to target our think tank. Seers are prophets, yes? I felt Rimbaud had us in mind with his demented collage of fantastical, nauseating images. It was creepy. First, literature, the line of work I've pursued.

Larnaca, 1 March 1879. Poetry disgusts me. My poems were the ulcerous seepage of reckless youth. I renounce them. The Sun, the bloody Sun, seeks vengeance for my insolence. Radiant beauty? No, Apollo is the deity of roughened skin, scorched eyes, deep torpor. I've traded up from poetry to carpentry. Tomorrow I jolt my workers with explosions to preempt mutinies. I must write my mother for a dagger. She is good for little else. All is desert here, vindictive, hardly indifferent. This island is alive with the spirit of death. Shakespeare knew this, for Othello is death. But I'll never read literature again. Shakespeare tells me nothing I do not already know. In Cyprus I'm in my element, an infernal Helios. My workers murder one another when they've not already dropped dead from typhus. I smile. Thank you, imperialist English bastards, for your intervention. I foresee another benighted takeover in 1974. By then, literature will be a bagatelle and my words vaporized. Fine by me.

Rimbaud was a loathsome brat. That cancerous leg was in keeping with his larger sensibility. Frankly, he got the leg he deserved.

He was also the world's greatest literary prodigy. What does this say about literature?

I translated a few more passages, each a prophetic gloss on the interests and personalities of the think tank. Having dumped on my own field, Rimbaud had lots to say about Darcy's passion, the animal kingdom.

Larnaca, 15 March 1879. Animals sob with grief because they are poor and outnumbered, except the locusts, who are many. In swarms they eat up this miserable island. Villagers must bag their quota or go to jail where they are forced to dine on—locusts! I sing the locust. The island is also terrified of snakes. But snakes I like, for I am one! The snake within guides my pen. I behold newly hatched sea turtles gobbled by predator birds, luminous dragonflies crunched by reptiles, noble mouflon slain for sport or stew, and melodious songbirds swallowed whole by locals. Snakes are wise, they approve.

No absinthe so I sip zivanía while scribbling in midnight heat. It moves my blood, branching out to extremities of hands, feet, and crotch. Resolved that I leave Cyprus as soon as I've sought out the shrine of Aphrodite and have drachmas in my pocket . . .

Larnaca, 16 March 1879. Just awakened from a stupor. The sun is up, must confront my hopeless workers. I renounced poetry and now renounce this accursed notebook. The snake within? I flattered myself. I'm a chickenshit. Must think this through . . .

Spirit of Apollo, I implore you. Corral the rare and worthy animals and let me sail with them for Mount Arafat, on a boat with a mind of its own as drunk as Noah, heading east in pursuit of the singing dolphins.

Did I once write such a poem? O futurity! Spare the rare animals, find sands safe for the sea turtles, free passage for the songbirds, an enclave for the noble mouflon. Let scorpions ring themselves with fire and die. Merde, do I have a conscience after all? Apollo, save me from conscience! I leave off this notebook for now.

I cannot read this passage without thinking of Darcy and, before him, Gerald Durrell, who sought enclaves for rare beasts and crossed the divide between thought and sensation. "O for a Life of Sensations rather than of Thoughts!" cried Keats, who wrote a superb sonnet about Mrs. Reynolds's cat. But Keats was a kindly and generous stripling who deserved to live. I'm not so sure about Rimbaud.

Here's a passage from the journal that seems to have Jasmine in mind. Rimbaud tells us what's for dinner. Bon appétit!

Larnaca, 21 March 1879. I'd rather eat myself than the fare they offer on this putrid island—small tough game, withered chickens, watery vegetables, and boiled mutton, thank you, Brits. I'll eat dirt, stones, coal, and iron, better for me. The earth produces its sap, its riverwater, its green blood. Romantic poets worshipped exotic harvests and flowers. I too wrote such a poem and asked if a flower, whether

rose or lily, is worth the excrement of a single seabird. Charming.
Cyprus is the denuded earth in an eternal season of Hell. Here I take
the nourishment of death.

If this strikes you as sour grapes, the lad has a point. Either no
food in a denuded Earth or the greasy carbs of the Brits? These must
be false alternatives, and I could see a fruitful collaboration of
Jasmine and Gayle on this matter of agriculture versus
desertification, if only Jasmine could move beyond her petty
jealousy. Yes, Jasmine's itch for Darcy was unreciprocated, as his
was for Gayle, as Gayle's for me. The heart hath its reasons even
within a think tank where one might expect that higher animals act
like adults.

Rimbaud and fellow poet Verlaine had an itch, more so a
passion, that landed Verlaine in jail after he took pistol shots at his
boy toy, who was surely asking for it. These felons were grand
écrivains, if amateurs in the fine art of murder. I hoped the fellows
of the Cyprus Think Tank would settle down and elude the damage
that biographers routinely inflict on their victims. My diplomatic
disposition and an affection I'd developed toward all the fellows,
even Darcy and Albert, make me disinclined to portray them
harshly. But from the beginning I was asking for good material, and
the annals of lust, jealousy, envy, and ambition provide it. If not on
the cosmic scale of *Othello* or Rimbaud, the fellows will be found
here and there popping up in these very annals.

I note that Rimbaud seemed capable of a change of heart, so surely
the fellows could overcome whatever gave them heartburn. I hoped
my memoir would not be a downer in the end but, at this moment
in the Cyprus saga, I could only sit back and wait for the sequel.

Chapter Eight

APHRODITE OUTED

It was late May, and Melusina and her team of divers were closing in on the Aphrodite carved by Pygmalion sometime when mythology intersected ancient history. Legend has it that he carved the gigantic marble statue by way of thanking Aphrodite for having turned his life-sized statue of Galatea into living flesh. To the extent the fellows of the think tank could suspend their own endeavors, they entered in not as divers but as onlookers, except Jasmine, who was the equal of Melusina as mermaid. We offered encouragement during the day and animated evening conversation at West End Restaurant's fish fry, where Melusina's divers were engaged in yet another rowdy Scrabble smackdown.

For my part I can dogpaddle well enough, so with a snorkel and underwater transceiver I monitored the goings-on at a depth of thirty feet as Melusina, Jasmine, and the divers, with oxygen tanks, transceivers, and underwater archeological equipment explored the ancient and now submerged viaduct that once connected the island with the mainland.

I stared down at the underwater choreography of my two fellows as they glided amid soldier fish, starfish, anemones, and octopuses. The latter intelligent but delicious creatures figure large in Cypriot pottery and painting, emblematic of swift adaptability to all that history flings their way. Not my metaphor but, like the octopus, Cyprus had been caught and eaten by poachers, despite tactics of evasion and camouflage. It was mesmerizing to watch pale Melusina and ebon Jasmine as they honed in on a protruding shelf of shale and, with the archeological version of a crowbar, set gently to pry it open.

When the underwater cloud of debris cleared, I beheld in astonishment a human hand in pink stone. The two women embraced one another and signaled thumbs up. I attached an enlargement lens to my snorkel and beheld a large marble hand that had not suffered the insults of time. It was fully intact. If it remained attached to an arm and the arm to a torso, and the torso was still in possession of its head, this would be one of the few wholly intact masterworks of antiquity.

And so it turned out to be. Over the next week the underwater team removed the silt encasement that had both buried and preserved the sculpture. Slowly the nude body of Aphrodite became visible, without doubt the greatest archeological discovery since King Tut's tomb, the Venus de Milo, and the Apollo Belvedere. But all these had deficits—King Tut's tomb had been vandalized by ancient grave robbers, the Venus de Milo was missing her arms, and the Apollo Belvedere his penis.

The international media were kept in the dark by the think tank until the Aphrodite was completely exhumed, cleaned, and mounted for the official unveiling. This event Melusina decided would take place on *Kataklysmós*, the annual celebration of Noah's catastrophic flood fifty days after Easter. Everybody takes to the sea and splashes others in a communal ritual of minor aggression and major flirtation. The festival is unique to Cyprus.

In the next week, we discussed the import of the discovery for Cyprus and the fame it would bring Melusina, already a celebrity but not unhappy at having her fame compounded.

"Frankly," said Albert, swallowing whole a luckless songbird over the objections of Jasmine, Gayle, and Darcy, and casting the beak aside, "I don't see the relevance to the fate of nations of an ancient piece of pink marble. Pygmalion's moment has passed, and nobody believes in Greek deities anymore. Do you still believe in Tinkerbell? *Oy*, let's clap our hands. Science has cast a dark cloud on this religious claptrap. Pagan religion is still religion. Good riddance."

Melusina cringed as she listened to the science nerd who had resolutely ignored her attempts at amorous brokerage, unwilling to engage in nocturnal pillow fights or even share a late night zivanía, and now scorning her life's work. Never before had she encountered someone so resistant. At first it had been a welcome challenge, but she soon came to find, as she would confess to me, the idea of copulation with him as tempting as getting it on with an axolotl.

"*Ja*, Albert, dump on my life's work. I am taking it. But art hath a use. My compatriot Schiller has said it best. It is only when politics is passing through the guts of the aesthetic that humanity will be surviving and flourishing."

I injected some of my reliable diplomacies. "Albert, please acknowledge that Pygmalion's Aphrodite is no Tinkerbell. She's solid marble and real, has waited millennia to play her hand. You have the promise of mirror neurons to overcome ethnic hatred. But it doesn't take a Greek Cypriot to delight in Aphrodite—Turkish Cypriots will cheer too. She represents another type of human bonding."

Throughout this debate Albert was glancing down at his cell phone and sweating. Exactly why will become clear. Suffice it for now to say that, when Melusina alluded to having her life's work dumped on by this potential Nobelist, he flinched.

Here is what Rimbaud has to say on the subject of Greek deities and mythic sensibility in *Cahier II*. This is the final entry made during his stay in Larnaca.

Larnaca, 2 May 1879. I once bit my sister's butt. I was consumed by buttocks from an early age, of either sex, old and young, fat and skinny. The Callipygian Venus I worship, her arse the epitome of beauty, the redemptive flesh. At night in this arid island I see her born again, white foam like the sea's ejaculate escorting her to shore on a half-shell. O for a return of the pagan blood, the Caryatids with their tears of sidereal gold! We need Phoebe and Endymion, Helen and Paris, and Venus, the Aphrodite of Cyprus. In futurity I see her pink sculpture unearthed. Thousands will join in worship at her shrine. I sense her presence now. My Aphrodite, are you somewhere in hiding? My alchemical charts tell that you lurk somewhere near Páphos, close to your first visitation.

So Rimbaud, the seer, as usual deranging our senses with equal amounts of visionariness and obscenity.

I'll skip ahead to the notebook's final entry about a year later, dated June 28, 1880, written in the Troödhitissa monastery, just a few days after he whacked a worker and fled the construction project. If the British authorities had pushed the monks to hand over the notebook, they would have made more work for themselves because this passage seems self-incriminating.

I once wrote that the seer must become monstrous, planting warts on his own face. Last week I planted a wart that can never be removed. I'm a monster. I regret it but feel no remorse. The bastard declined to follow orders. True, I know nothing about construction, but an order is an order and I went into a rage, sorry about that. Now, hiding out in this dreadful monastery, I need the piano I begged my mother for back in Charleville after I left off poetry forever. She relented only when I carved a keyboard on the dining room table. I'll play "Rage Over a Lost Penny" over and over again, and watch the monks dance like spastic puppets. See, I have humor. But what I truly need are celestial harmonies, patterns of sound to escort me to the stars, like Bach's Well-Tempered or Mozart's great sonata in A minor or Beethoven's Opus 111. These earthlings are a true trinity. How can they be fucking Germans? Too difficult for an amateur like me to play, but I can read the scores like any other language.

Ah Verlaine! You sent a bullet into my wrist and I forgave you. Had you been a better shot and sent it through my skull, the outcome would have been happier, I dead and you headed for the guillotine—two monsters out of combat before we could commit more visionary verse, an abomination in the eyes of the sun god. Sixteen bars of Bach's French suites are worth more than all my Illuminations. He was a true god, I only a minor Satan. I'll spend the rest of my life in expiation not for murder but for writing. Here I'll stay until I can make a break for a steamer heading to the East where money can be made. If ever this notebook falls into the hands of some unfortunate bookish hack, let him know not to set his eyes on a higher calling, because writers are misguided lunatics, rightly doomed.

Bookish hack? Ouch. Go back to Hell, Monsieur Rimbaud.

Melusina agreed to call a press conference where she would announce her discovery in time for *Kataklysmós,* and she insisted on managing the whole affair according to her own theatrical aesthetic. This meant a pagan dance of hamadryads and satyrs, the fabrication of a Garden of Adonis, and Melusina herself barefoot in her white toga, with a broad Tyrian purple stripe around the border, beneath which she planned to wear only a thong and two Band-Aids.

I notified the international press, which had edited Cyprus out of the picture after reunification briefly made page one. The airports at Larnaca and Nicosia became busy once again when what we used to call "reporters"—now "fake-news managers"—were flown in to cover the event. This was a cushy assignment because all hoped to see a three-dimensional Botticelli. In his masterpiece, the painter had done full service to Aphrodite's frontal torso but ignored her backside, ironically the body part on which her fame is suspended. Each fake-news manager hoped to be the first to beam Aphrodite's backside to the world.

Melusina would make the announcement atop the island of Yeronisos within the ruins of the latter-day Roman atrium. This presented a problem to camera crews because there is no accommodating port on the island. When the crew from the reconstituted USSR tried to forge the two hundred yards from shoreline to island, they top-loaded their rowboat and both equipment and fake-news managers ended up in the drink. Fortunately, Melusina's divers fished them out, but the crew knew their humiliation had been recorded by all other camera crews. And Emperor Putin routinely executed anybody—athletes, writers, generals—who disgraced the USSR.

Others had more foresight and hired local helicopters, some more airworthy than others, to carry them to Melusina's pavilion. There stood an imposing twenty-foot statue whose veil would soon be drawn aside. I'll leave the logistics of hauling the seven-ton statue and setting it upright to your imagination but, in a word, it wasn't easy.

"World," began Melusina, confronting the three hundred members of the fake-news press corps who had barely survived transport to the island, and brushing aside a persistent hovering dragonfly. She was standing beneath the statue and looking as if she were herself the embodiment of Aphrodite, her toga dangerously close to parting in what would have been this planet's greatest disclosure of personal nudity since Janet Jackson's at the 2004 Super Bowl. "It is giving me unalloyed pleasure to be announcing the discovery and reclamation of Pygmalion's vanished statue of Aphrodite, left on the very island—resplendent Cyprus—where she has come ashore millennia ago. My own role in this discovery is being, well, pivotal, but I am not pulling it off without the assistance of my glam partner, Jasmine Ivory, who has taken time from her own project of reducing the Cypriot waistline a hand to lend. I am also sharing the stage with the pan-Cypriot team of divers—both Greeks and Turks—whose occasional squabbles over Scrabble always have stopped short of homicide. Take a bow—Volkan Akbaba! Androkles Christodoulides! Kudret Sakarya! Kallistratos Paphitis! Cumhur Yilmoz! Cletus Constantinides! Berkant Aksoy! Sophronios Kaimakliotis! Tolga Ahmad! Milos Lakkotripis! Akmet Pehliv! Takis Kayalis! Abdullah Karaduman! Topher Agathangelou!"

As their names were called, each waddled out to wave and collect his fifteen seconds of fame, still equipped in his scuba suit for authenticity. Then Takis Kayalis grabbed the mike and demanded to know if the Ministry of Finance had increased their minimum wage.

"They tend to it, I'm sure," said Melusina, like a concerned medical intern. "Now the moment . . . Takis, pull the veil!" There was a collective gasp as the veil fell away, revealing the triumphant nudity of the world's most radiant sculpture, twenty feet of imposing pink marble standing in monumental mockery of us mortals, who could only gape at the exquisitely carved frame that somehow made Michelangelo's David puny and tortured by contrast, and merely male.

"Art historians will be rewriting their histories of Greek sculpture in light of my—I mean *our*—find. Fully intact, this Aphrodite is having the arms, hands, fingers, and toes missing in her successors. Fully fleshed from all angles instead of betraying the frontal obsession of the archaic sculptors who have come later. And not protecting her breasts and pudendum, she is outstretching her arms in a manner inviting. Of the minute anatomical detail you are noting—the hair around the nipples, the parted lips expressive of erotic hunger, and the audacious backside, for which even Rimbaud would lack an adequate word-hoard. *Natürlich*, I am seeing many of you part ranks to take a look. You are not disappointed. The descriptor *callipygian* is being well earned. Observe also that she has been painted! Miraculously, some paint is surviving. Her eyes, an emerald green of malachite and natural basic carbonate, and her archaic braids and pubic hair, a luminous red of cinnabar and natural mercuric sulfide."

I'd interject that Melusina was incapable of speaking without sexualizing her discourse, even when the subject wasn't the world's most sumptuous naked woman.

"There is being only one departure from ideal anatomical realism," she continued. "Look close and you are seeing that her toes are webbed. Pygmalion has known that Aphrodite was a creature of the sea, a first-rate swimmer, and could on a giant oyster half-shell adroitly balance. Much of her DNA has been mermaid. Now, I've timed this to coincide with the celebration unique to Cyprus, the *Kataklysmós*, so that all bathers splashing water on one another do so with greater ardor, remembering that it has been Aphrodite who first commanded us to be making love, not war. Greeks and Turks must be discovering the invisible bonds that are uniting them beyond the petty divisions of post-pagan history. Bring on the Bacchantes before we are disrobing and heading for the beach!"

Nine NYU undergraduates from the Tisch School of the Arts had been conscripted to enact a pagan rite of consecration, choreographed by Melusina. Catching the morning rays on her forehead, Aphrodite warmed to the movements of the adoring young mortals, who would be performing other Paphian rites down the beach that evening. I watched as Jasmine eagerly approached Melusina.

"You made quite a splash, Melusina," she said. "Even Albert looked impressed."

They took hands facing one another. Then Melusina whirled Jasmine round and round, as if the skinny African-American were a toy doll. The press corps surrounded them just like the movies when Fred Astaire and Ginger Rogers stole the show. Aphrodite was for a time herself upstaged.

"Let's swim!" Melusina exclaimed, as the fake-news managers took leave for other cataclysmic events. Aphrodite presided over all, with a lone guard and a ticket-taker who would be posted indefinitely. The entire think tank sped off in the Land Rover down to Pétra toú Romíou, where bathers wcrc already engaged in splashing one another. Others were earnestly swimming three times around the rock formation to regain their virginities, soon to be lost yet again in a beach party that tempted the most pious to forget their vows. Albert looked away from the couplings that dotted the beach here and there. He, Darcy, and I retained our male modesty with swimming trunks, while Melusina, Jasmine, and Gayle stripped bare and jumped in. We engaged in horseplay. Melusina splashed Jasmine who splashed Darcy who splashed Gayle who splashed me. That left me to splash Albert, but I declined and splashed somebody not in our company.

This was none other than Armide, the volunteer paired off with Renaud in Albert's mirror-neuron experiment. Not that she was naked—she wore an ankle-length lime-green burkini. She was once again against the grain of modern Turkish Cypriot women, who eschew burkinis. Except for sunglasses, her face was now bare, and I was startled to see that she was the spitting image of Muslim supermodel Bella Hadid.

Her presence at the ritual splashing underscored the import of Melusina's discovery, as Muslims the world over joined others in celebrating the Aphrodite. Mainland Turks have no problem with the Ancient Greeks, who they feel share little with the post-Ottoman low-rent Merry Greeks of today. After all, Asia Minor has many of the world's best-preserved Greek temples and sculpture. Turks can claim the Aphrodite of Pygmalion is every bit as much their own, since she could hardly be the sole property of contemporary Greeks who absurdly claim kinship with great Agamemnon.

"Mister Beasley, like, I splash you back!" Armide cried in Turkish, laughing. Her body concealed by wetted fabric was sexier than bare flesh, and I felt a slight throb. At first I didn't know Renaud was eyeing us from a small abutment one hundred feet away. Though he and Armide continued their smoldering threats in experimental sessions, I'd learn that the two had begun to assume the intimacy that only seasoned combatants can feel. At the moment I didn't know the peril in which I was placing myself. Nor, I think, did Armide.

Darcy took to splashing Gayle with gusto, while she deflected the spray and instead of splashing back continued her futile splashes at me. Perhaps she felt the yellow bile while Armide and I augmented our mutual splashery. I guessed that beneath the burkini lay a body of exquisite proportions. I had to admit that the body parts of our three female think-tank fellows were, in different ways, exemplary, and that those of Albert, Darcy, and me were lamentable. We were jellyfish, in keeping with the cliché that males of our species can let themselves go and still feel capable of acquiring mates, while females must maintain vigils against time and gravity.

Jasmine and Melusina dove under and, through ripples, I could see them in a lascivious underwater embrace. This confirmed my hunch. Jasmine was getting over her senseless crush on Darcy and finding something more welcoming in Sapphic embrace. And Melusina, in keeping with queer erotics and maybe forsaking polyamory, was now focused on a single woman.

When they surfaced I announced that we should all adjourn to La Cavocle, a fourteenth-century manor near Palaepaphos that had been converted into a hotel with one of the few three-star restaurants in Cyprus. Armide thought this a good idea, as she, Melusina, and I conversed in Turkish and waded ashore.

It was then that Renaud announced his presence, standing on a ledge in a Speedo, arms akimbo, eyeing Armide and me. Renaud may have come over as a bit of a schlub, but there was no denying that he exerted male territoriality at this moment. I asked in Greek if he would like to join us for meze at La Cavocle. Declining at first— "You seem to be doing well enough without me"—he relented when Armide threatened him with a sharp oyster shell.

"I will, like, spill your guts, motherfucker," she said in Turkish, and Renaud tactfully relented, not knowing exactly what she had said but sensing it was scary.

I will not narrate the dinner. Assume that libations were made, that the broken chain of flirtation persisted in some measure, but that realignments were emerging. And Armide and Renaud, at opposite ends of the table, postponed mutual murder for the time being.

— Chapter Nine —

THE INVADERS

In a sensible division of labor, Darcy, Melusina, and I headed north to Béllapais to seek out traces of the Durrell brothers, while Gayle graciously asked Jasmine to team up with her in confronting the problem of Cypriot desertification. Whatever jealousy Jasmine may have felt over Darcy's obvious preference for Gayle was set aside for a cause less trivial. Albert, who had been even more fretful and preoccupied in recent days, stayed behind to continue collecting data on his volunteers. Gayle and Jasmine told me subsequently of their quest and near catastrophe, but I admit to fabricating some plausible dialogue here and there.

Gayle was set on making oases out of deserts, while Jasmine recognized that farmers markets do not spring up of a sudden in the Sahara. Perhaps rainfall could be teased out of wispy clouds. Gayle had studied cloud seeding in Oregon, where rainfall is all too abundant. With help from a high school chemistry textbook, she hit on a formula as yet untested that might bring about the Oregonization of other atmospheres on planet Earth. She applied for a patent and looked forward to disproving the many scoffers. Cloud seeding has had a poor track record, on a par with Native American ritual rainmaking.

Gayle kept a quote from William Blake in her cargo vest: "Hungry clouds swag on the deep." How does one convince small cirrus clouds to swag with water molecules? At first glance her formula seemed simplistic, but science sometimes finds its most elegant solutions in intuitions that cut through muddle, as if to make less prescient scientists ask, "Why didn't *I* think of that?" The formula consisted of Morton table salt, Johnson & Johnson baby powder, and Armato dry ice, plus a secret ingredient to be disclosed in time. With a loan from the American Confederation of Cloud Seeders and a subsidy from Soros, she fabricated and shipped two tons of the compound from Portland to Páphos before leaving for Cyprus.

"Jasmine, come along and heave this stuff out the tail end of the Cessna. If all goes according to plan, we'll create a monsoon."

"Will do, Gayle, but please no fancy twists, turns, and tailspins, like that dragonfly over there. Want your monsoon mixed with barf?"

"Not a problem. Good fertilizer."

Jasmine was terrified at the prospect of another flight with Gayle and, before departure the morning of June twenty-first, took two Valiums.

"Have you checked the fuel? Is your compound too heavy for the Cessna? Is there anything more evolved than a shovel?"

Gayle gave assurances and the two boarded the plane, which cleared the runway with a good twenty meters to spare. Up, up, and away they flew over the Páphos forest to the Tróödos mountains to the Pendadháktylos summit, and then over Kyrenia, where— through a series of textings to the think-tank fellows, who were then driving to the House of Durrell—they looked down and waved at us as we exited the Rover for a moment. Then they took a sharp turn north. Every time Gayle texted us, the Cessna underwent a turbulent jerk, triggering Jasmine's air sickness. Gayle explained to her companion, greener by the minute, that the winds favored a seeding close to the Turkish border. The clouds would then head toward Cyprus, thanks to dependable meteorological currents. Cyprus often complains of getting preowned Turkish weather.

They were within thirty miles of the Turkish coastline when Gayle spotted some small cirrus clouds and sped off in pursuit. "Now!" she cried, "Start shoveling!" Jasmine did so, simultaneously tossing her cookies out the emergency exit. No proof that vomit betters the odds of rain formation, but within minutes the formerly modest cirrus began congealing into giant hungry clouds that swagged off in the direction of Cyprus.

"Good, seems to be working. Keep shoveling."

"Please don't tell Melusina that I barfed."

Jasmine continued shoveling the Morton table salt, Johnson & Johnson baby powder, Armato dry ice, and secret ingredient out the emergency exit with gratifying results. Eventually she pitched all the compound on board that day.

"That'll do for now," said Gayle. "We return tomorrow with another dose. From cirrus to cumulonimbus in minutes—better than I'd hoped for." She turned around to bump fists with Jasmine, sending the Cessna into a roll.

At this point the aircraft was caught in a sudden updraft that took it out of Gayle's control altogether. The two rainmakers looked to their sides and beheld four jets. They were close enough for Gayle to see a grinning pilot's gesticulations, one hand pointing down toward Turkey, the other indicating a slit throat. Gayle nodded and the jets accompanied them to a small airport in Mersin. Her last communication to us was "We're surrounded by four Turkish F-16C Fighting Falcons. *Sauve qui peux!*"

On the ground Jasmine leaned over and retched at the approaching pilots, who dodged the splatter.

"At least they're sorta handsome," said Gayle.

All four spoke excellent English. "For love of Allah," said one, pointing his rusted AK-47 from one to the other, "what are you ladies up to?"

Gayle spoke with the self-assurance of a tree-hugger. "We're saving Cyprus from desertification and we'll be back tomorrow with another load of our special compound."

"Sure thing, and I'm saving Turkey from being eaten with stuffing and cranberry sauce," said a smart-aleck pilot. The others joined in laughter at the old joke.

"Really, ladies," said another, "admit that you are American spies. Seems weird, gotta say, since Turkey and the U.S. of A. signed a frigging mutual nonaggression treaty over the objections of disgraced President Trump, and we send all those hookahs to the East Village. Allow us to inspect your cargo."

The Rainfall Superpowder had all been dispersed but the Cessna still had Soros foundation retrofitting and was in reality empowered to do some high-level spying. What the Turks chose not to believe was that the only technology Gayle and Jasmine had deployed was an Ace hardware shovel.

"In the name of Allah, what's this?" asked one, holding the shovel soiled with vomit.

Gayle was irritated. "That's for digging aerial latrines, meathead." Her environmental activism was getting the better of her.

"Cool it," whispered Jasmine. "Let them have their way, up to a point. And *meathead* was put out to pasture long ago."

"We are seizing this spy plane and you ladies will confront a military tribunal. In your lingo, *Tell it to the judge.*"

"I'm a chef," said Jasmine. "Please allow me to fix dinner for six. Does this airport have a pantry?"

"Sorry, lady, we'll do the cooking. Stale pita and tap water for you. We drink bottled water for fear of typhus."

Gayle carried some extra baggage because of an environmentalist's love of yams and craft beer, but Jasmine was a vision in skin and bones, and a jailhouse diet would never do. Within two hours they had fingers printed, mugs shot, retinas scanned, and DNA retrieved from saliva. They were booked into the local prison in Mersin, which outstripped medieval dungeons in darkness, discomfort, and vermin, and were locked into adjoining five-by-seven cells.

"Human Rights Watch will hear of this," warned Gayle.

"The NAACP will take you creeps to task," cried Jasmine.

A few hours later, manacled and grumpy, they were pulled from their cells to appear before a Turkish magistrate of indefinite powers and jurisdiction. He wore a djellaba stained with fig juice and slumgullion. To economize on space, the courtroom doubled as a Turkish bath, so our fellows were surrounded by sweaty naked elderly males who jumped into steamy pools while life sentences and decapitations were routinely meted out. *Alice in Wonderland* had nothing on this. The magistrate spoke only Turkish, so the two women, better versed in Greek, didn't know exactly what the charges were. The magistrate's frowns and mutterings implied a capital offense.

"Could we have a court-appointed lawyer, please?" interjected Gayle. The magistrate didn't understand the question, but one of the pilots advanced to serve as interpreter.

"You are being charged with espionage and worse, most unladylike behavior. The punishments for the latter include flagellation, stoning, decapitation, or tickling, depending on the pleasure of the court. And once again, what were you doing with that Ace hardware shovel?"

He translated Gayle's reply to the magistrate. "We're rainmakers, highly regarded in many cultures. We were administering Rainfall Superpowder. I've applied for the patent . . . but I won't give you the formula."

These words amused the magistrate. "You are as likely to make rain as I am to grant clemency. But show me evidence of rain and you are free to depart as soon as we've downloaded all your data and you've given us this . . . formula. We have some desertification issues of our own."

"The formula is as carefully guarded as Coca-Cola's," replied Gayle, to the consternation of Jasmine, who was anxious to get out of there.

Lo! The courtroom was all at once shaken by lightning, thunder, and rainfall of unprecedented volume. Water spewed into the court chamber, raising in seconds the pool's water three feet, and forcing the magistrate to hold his robe above his Turkish undies.

At this moment in splashed a guard who handed a note to the magistrate. He read it and intoned, "We see there is good evidence for the efficacy of Rainfall Superpowder. Not only is Southern Turkey drenched but all the former Turkish Republic of Northern Cyprus is enjoying a monsoon, albeit it has washed away many antiquities and pensioners. You are free to depart if, in the next five minutes, you divulge the formula."

Gayle was handed a piece of paper and a Paper Mate #2 Sharpwriter. "Oh well, you might as well have it." She wrote down three items: Morton table salt, Johnson & Johnson baby powder, and Armato dry ice. The pilot translated, and the magistrate, apparently knowing little about chemistry, seemed impressed and decided against decapitation. A military cordon escorted the two to their Cessna, whose wheels were encrusted with sand from the overflow. The plane's data had all been downloaded onto antiquated USB flash drives, and the invaders were free to taxi down the runway, now eroded by numerous rivulets.

As they prepared for takeoff, Jasmine asked Gayle why she had divulged the formula.

"But I didn't. That would mean telling them two parts this, four parts that, three parts this. Without the right proportions and in the right sequence, the stuff won't work. True science is found in the details. And one detail I didn't even write down, the catalytic agent for the other three."

"What is it?"

"Hydrochlorothiazide."

"Hydrochlorothiazide?"

"Yes, Jasmine, hydrochlorothiazide, the world's most prescribed diuretic!"

Chapter Ten

THE ROAD TO BÉLLAPAIS

I'll back up a bit to the departure of Melusina, Darcy, and me for Lawrence Durrell's house at Béllapais, where he stayed from 1953 to 1956. In this house he wrote *Justine*, the first volume of *The Alexandria Quartet*, which won his fame and instilled in me at an early age a love of the exotic. We had taken Armide along for her intimate knowledge of the North and customs of Turkish Cypriots. She would act as a go-between. I took the wheel of the Rover and got lots of counsel from my passengers about which way to turn and why I should drive faster.

Darcy held a small Turkish phrase book and spoke nonsense whenever we encountered a local, even though Armide, Melusina, and I were all proficient in the language. As you know, Darcy's passion for animals echoed Durrell's younger brother Gerald, who outstayed his welcome at Béllapais, encaging diverse specimens of the island's wildlife on the earthen floor. Locals thought admission could be charged, as at a zoo. Lawrence had himself encountered a domestic animal on his first visit to the house—a large heifer unaccountably chewing its cud in the living room. The real estate agent, crafty Sabri the Turk written up vividly in *Bitter Lemons*, clicked his tongue in classist disdain of locals who cohabited with their reeking animals.

Melusina accompanied us to check out the condition of Cypriot antiquities damaged during the Turkish occupation. Wearing little more than Aphrodite, she sat in the back seat with her archeological notebooks and camera. Her mission was to extend the Archeological Preservation Initiative to antiquities in the North, many weathering in the harsh Cypriot climate and now bearing fewer antique runes than the ideologically inspired gashes by Muslim Turks, who suspected all runes to have been tainted by Christianity. Cyprus reunification eased this desecration of vulnerable antiquities, but there were still many to find, keep off the black market, and preserve. One means of preservation was a virtual-reality device posing as cheap night-vision goggles, which made midnight looters imagine they were unearthing chiseled marble instead of the petrified dung that was in fact lying on their shovels.

Hearing that the house had undergone distressing renovations since Durrell's departure, I asked the Soros foundation to purchase it outright, send away the current owners, and restore it faithfully to what Durrell had left behind in 1956, fleeing the island when ethnic violence was on the rise. The foundation was happy to oblige and took seriously my suggestions of what to do with the house later on.

As we approached Béllapais, Darcy got on our nerves, flinging his arms and lecturing on sites and local history about which we knew more than he. And before we could complete our quest for the House of Durrell he insisted we detour to the enclosure near Stavrós tis Psókas where we'd find a mouflon around every abutment, as well as a ruined monastery with a cross known for curing scabies.

"We Brits get the credit for every mouflon. Only twenty left when we took the reins in 1878, now a thousand. There should be many thousands. Armide, you bloody Turks shot them for stew and sport. No wonder they're shy. Look over there."

Armide did not understand English well enough to catch the accusation. But sure enough a mouflon was making itself scarce. We had a glimpse of its famed horns and white backside as the startled beast headed down a trail amidst the cedar forest. Darcy took off in orgasmic pursuit. We could hear him aping the resonate *baa* of the mouflon. Striding after him, we heard a distant fracas through the forest and, after a few minutes, came across a most remarkable scene.

Darcy had cornered the mouflon in an enclosed ridge and seemed to be conversing with him amicably. "Baa." *Baa.* "Baa?" *Baa.* "Baa!" He had already decided the name of this particular mouflon was Bragadino, much to the displeasure of Armide, who growled through her niqad at mention of the name. She honored the memory of Mustafa, the Turkish general who stuffed the mutilated body of Bragadino with straw upon failing to honor his pledge of safe passage after the siege of Famagusta in 1571. But Bragadino the mouflon seemed to respond well to this name and permitted Darcy to caress his huge curled horns.

He had brought along a supply of testosterone patches, engineered by biochemists at Berkeley, and was resolved to boost the testosterone levels of male mouflon, hoping this would multiply the mouflon population by a factor of three in only three years, given a gestation period of five months. The mating season was traditionally November, but Darcy had a plan for making mouflon more like humans in having no particular predilection for fucking only in November. He attached the patch to Bragadino's scrotum and planned to hire locals to seek out all male mouflon with the same biologic intervention at hand. Male mouflon would be in perpetual rut—an infirmity inflicted on male humans that may in part account for the eight billion Homo "sapiens" now destroying planet Earth.

Darcy and Bragadino bade farewell, friends forever. He told the beast to be fruitful and multiply, and the four of us hit the road again for Kyrenia. Melusina applauded this scheme of mouflon testosterone enhancement since it was in keeping with her polyamorous agenda—fucking instead of fighting. Hers was a vision of sex as the Taj Mahal that D. H. Lawrence made it out it to be, according to Lawrence Durrell, who had credentials of his own in this field.

With her signature handshake, Melusina crushed Darcy's metacarpals and began talking about sex. "I have tried out polyamory after reading Fourier. He was a utopian *Dummkopf* who has prophesied that humans would someday be growing seven feet tall, the salt sea would be turning to pink lemonade, and women would be having four husbands all at once. I had only one at the time and felt envious of these future females—I was twenty-three—so I have broached the subject with my husband, a young lawyer in contract law, who confessed that he has had a roving eye like me and marriage felt too, well, contractual. So an ad in the *Berlin Sun* we placed, asking if other couples might be wanting to explore what you Americans call *swinging*. Please reply in handwriting. We promised light refreshments. Little we expected an avalanche of replies. We triaged them by graphology—what was the handwriting revealing about the applicants? We soon had so many encounters that we began a list, with German equivalents of *needies*, *dullards*, and *stinkeroos* for never again. There have been some standouts—the German for *mammy-jammers* and *killer-dillers*."

"Weren't you afraid of VD? And what about jealousy? Out of fashion?" asked a skeptical Darcy.

"We practiced safe sex, like shadow sex where people have acted out their encounters by handmade shadows on the walls. We had a baby daughter, Mariele, and protected her from primal scenes. So some modesty there was. After a couple of years my husband has found somebody he liked better, and they have broken the rules by seeing each other alone. We had a cordial divorce and I am finding another mate, this time not a mere husband. We continued polyamory but with a difference: *No more light refreshments!* It isn't that I am liking sex so much, it's the adventure of finding out the most intimate thing you can ever know about another human being within minutes, and then it's 'bye-bye.' I have found myself toward strangers warmly inclined, unless they are being crypto-fascist Americans who voted for Trump. Then I am wanting to kill them."

"You've never mentioned your daughter before," I said.

"Mariele and I are texting each other every day. She's fourteen now and looks just like me. But she says her 'self-realization' is crying out for a life different from her mom's. Could we please do away with self-realization? She's living at a prestigious Berlin middle school for girls and is expecting to be a viral soccer star when she grows up. I am loving the girl and hoping she redirects her passions. But passions direct themselves, moms have little say. I'd never tell her to go the way of polyamory. An acquired taste. I also had a career in archeology, and fooling around with strangers began too many hours of the day to take up. My new mate and I felt we had more important goals—he was earnest about bee-keeping right there in Berlin—so we split up. I still feel that love is triumphing over all, despite—well, there's some counterevidence. Depending on how things go with Jasmine, I may reconsider polyamory."

Like Darcy, Melusina insisted on many stops en route to the House of Durrell, including a quick midafternoon tour of Saint Hilarion Castle, where one hundred rooms are accessible, while the one-hundred-and-first is a lost enchanted garden where Aphrodite tucked a treasure. When the castle closed at four thirty, Melusina hid in an alcove, hoping over our protestations to search after hours for the treasure. We waited patiently in the Rover until castle guards carried her out by all fours. I reached in my pocket for the Soros's contingency euros, and the four of us drove on.

We soon reached the large box house of Lawrence Durrell, overlooking the famed Tree of Idleness, Béllapais Abbey, the castle of Kyrenia, and the hills of Buffavento beyond. Bringing the Rover to a halt, we looked up from the landmark water pump next to the house and witnessed a darkening of the sky quite unusual on this sun-drenched isle.

An ancient Turkish Cypriot woman dressed in black approached with a giant key to the massive carved doors. "Mister Beasley, this house is haunted," she whispered in Turkish.

The thunder now underway forced me to read her lips. She was pleased that, at my request, the Soros foundation had removed all additions to the structure postdating Durrell's departure. But she whispered that they didn't remove the ghosts. "I hear them at night. I watch the house—I'm paid for it—but I never go inside. May Allah protect and preserve you!"

Her words gave Armide the creeps. She was already creeped out, sensing throughout our journey that we were being tailed. The macrocosm, now issuing thunder and lightning, didn't help. "We should listen to her. Let's call this thing off. Like, what do you expect to find anyway?"

For his part, Darcy hadn't caught on to enough Turkish to understand. "Did she just say this house is overrated?"

"No, haunted."

I took the iron key, as long as my forearm, thrust it into the pistol-spring lock, and pushed the portals, which creaked like the sound track for *Inner Sanctum*, a fifties radio horror show. The foyer was huge, the ceiling high, the wooden beams of Anatolian timber enormous and assertive.

"I am loving this place!" exclaimed Melusina. "Let's explore."

The large windows, "fretted with wooden slats of faintly Turkish design," as Durrell put it, gave enough light for us to walk cautiously down the hallway that led to the back of the house and the garden, with the imposing trees we'd viewed from the air. We found a large door and staircase leading to rooms upstairs and the balcony that Durrell designed, where the view of Béllapais Abbey and environs leading down to the sea was a marvel, now all the more dramatic because of the darkening sky and swagging clouds.

"Fine," I said. "But this place asks that something happen." I had planned this for months, rehearsing my words in a mirror, and hoped my companions would take fire. "I'll evoke the shades of Rimbaud, Lawrence Durrell, Gerald Durrell, and, if we're lucky, Shakespeare. They'll be our visionary company and perform for us. e. e. cummings reminds us that death is no parenthesis, and my hero Walter Pater asks, 'How shall we pass most swiftly from point to point, and be present always at the focus where the greatest number of vital forces unite in their purest energy?' Let's take him to heart here."

"I have heard that rhetoric about burning with a 'hard gemlike flame.' It came over pretty well in German," said Melusina. "Assistant professors of archeology at Göttingen and Heidelberg have quoted it to be getting into my pants. They have not needed to be working so hard. But Bart, I'm eager for the ghosts of Shakespeare, Rimbaud, and the Durrell brothers. Go ahead, rub the bottle."

It was then that the rains came, vindictively. We converged in the center of the living room as lights went out and shutters began banging. We felt a resonant thump from outside and rushed to the front casement to behold our Rover smashed beneath a fallen eucalyptus. "Doesn't matter," I said. "Gayle and Jasmine will be here soon with a replacement."

With desert soil unprepared to absorb such an onslaught, flash floods swept all over Northern Cyprus, the area earlier occupied by Turkish forces. The clouds finished dumping their load just as they reached the 1974 border with the South, which, after the fact, was read by some as proof that the gods favored the North, giving it much needed rain. Others thought it proof the gods favored the South, sparing it drownings and mudslides. I myself didn't believe in any gods and thought it good evidence that Gayle had outstripped Kurt Vonnegut's brother, who discovered a method for producing rain but whose first name nobody knows.

— *Chapter Eleven* —

THE IMPERSONATORS

Gayle and Jasmine had a bumpy return to Cyprus, riding out the maelstrom they had themselves created. They managed a squishy landing at the Nicosia airport, rented a Rover, and headed for Béllapais to join us for the week I had booked the House of Durrell. The journey by land was bumpy because flash floods were sweeping away roadways where mudslides had not already covered them. The storm had shut down the grid for most of Northern Cyprus, and citizens were plowing into each other at intersections, no doubt exiting their wrecks to loot nearby talismanic Byzantine icons. Emergency crews were at work. Because the island has had so little rain over the millennia, Cypriots are dim about what to do when it presents in buckets. For her part, Gaia was suffering an extreme case of urinary incontinence.

When Gayle and Jasmine approached the House of Durrell, they saw the hillside bestrewn with fallen eucalyptuses and the flattened Rover. A few villagers crouched beneath the still standing Tree of Idleness to watch the unprecedented spectacle and fret over the fate of zivanía production. Festooned again in her finest toga with purple stripe, Melusina pulled open the huge portals to welcome the returning heroes. But before the archeologist could embrace her girlfriend, Jasmine, hardly breathing and nauseous, fell on the floor, while Gayle seemed little the worse for wear.

"Join the party!" exclaimed Melusina, gesturing into the large foyer where we were all gathered in the candlelight.

"Quite a party, but there are some guys here I don't know," said Gayle while Jasmine rallied and stood upright.

"Jasmine and Gayle," I said, gesturing and bowing to the three strangers, "I'd like you to meet Arthur Rimbaud, Lawrence Durrell, and Gerald Durrell. You may call them Art, Larry, and Gerry."

"Arthur Rimbaud, Lawrence Durrell, Gerald Durrell? Surely you are kidding!" said Gayle. She and Jasmine stared at the three greats, who had just arrived by separate carriages in the middle of the maelstrom. It was uncanny. Rimbaud had his trademark radiant-blue eyes; Lawrence Durrell, his big nose; and Gerald Durrell, his handsome and gracious frame. Gerald was the most welcoming of the three shades. He was fairly tall, with a trimmed beard, wearing a dinner jacket, and bearing a live, well-behaved gerbil on his left arm while extending his right hand for a hearty shake.

"Many thanks for the catastrophe, Gayle and Jasmine," he laughed. "Fortunately, animals are better than humans in natural disasters. That tsunami last month saved the sea turtles, and other beasties scampered uphill to safety. Allow me to introduce my older brother, Larry, who imagines he is also wiser."

At five foot three, Lawrence Durrell reminded many of a dwarf satyr. He had none of Gerald's good looks. Most observers felt a gap between his diminutive physical appearance and the impassioned, inquiring, yet world-weary voice of Darley, narrator of *The Alexandria Quartet*. He was wearing a large fedora, maybe to draw attention away from his unseemly nose.

"Delighted," he said to the two women, sizing them up. "Gayle, you remind me somewhat of my heroine Clea, and Jasmine, you are faintly redolent of Justine. But mysteries of identity eclipse such simple identifications, yes? Justine and Clea are but paper fabrications. You are flesh and blood, and enticingly so, I must say." Lawrence Durrell was already confirming what his biographers said about his inveterate lechery. "Now allow me to introduce Art," he said, swallowing the "t" in deference to French pronunciation.

"Never call me *Art*, monsieur," snarled Rimbaud. "Either I am Arthur or I is another." At five foot eight and thin to the point of wasting away, he pierced the dimly lit room with those preternaturally blue eyes. His face was somehow both cherubic and satanic. At about thirty-two he was wearing the same outfit as in the iconic 1871 photograph by Étienne Carjat taken when he was seventeen—a jacket with broad lapels, a vest tightly buttoned, short dark double-pronged cravat askew to his left, and an uneven stiff collar, with an expression defiant, peevish, and penetrating. To judge by the odor, he had never had his attire cleaned. He was smoking hashish in a long clay pipe. "*Enchanté*," he said blandly to the two women and declined to extend a hand. We all stood around for a moment as if to ask, Now what?

Let me break in here to assure you that these three were not ghosts. They were also not holograms. And none of us fellows was wearing a virtual reality gizmo. No, I had asked the Soros foundation to offer large stipends to actors who made a living on impersonations—one-person shows with as much dramatic enactment as can be achieved within a monologue. I personally deplore one-person shows but guessed the art form might be just the ticket here, as claustrophobic monologue might give way to wide-ranging spontaneous dialogue.

You'd have thought the actor who played Gerald Durrell would have trouble rounding up an audience, given his lower ranking on the scale of literary greats. But with the growth of environmental awareness and a sense of humor superior to his depressive alcoholic older brother or the dour ex-poet Rimbaud, he had the greatest success of the three. There was also the charming BBC production, *The Durrells in Corfu*, which raised his standing, a fictionalized account of what was already fictional in Gerald's rendering of his childhood in Corfu. His lightweight screeds sold well while Lawrence's serious tomes went out of print.

In all three instances the actors so cohabited with their subjects that they were trapped in their personae, the legendary fate of Jonathan Winters struggling to escape roles he played. It soon became clear to all that the actor playing Lawrence Durrell truly believed that he had himself penned *The Alexandria Quartet*. He spoke the lilting cadences and erudite diction of the Anglo-Indian writer. Each actor had undergone a legal name change, so that Lawrence Durrell was now played by Lawrence Durrell, not Kaleb Kipling; Arthur Rimbaud by Arthur Rimbaud, not Dartagnon Descoteaux; and Gerald Durrell by Gerald Durrell, not Herschel Humperdinck.

My motive in bringing together these impersonators was pretty selfish. I hoped the spirit of the actual writers would be communicated to me, enlivening my dreams and reinvigorating my prose. Not far behind this was the salvation of Cyprus and maybe even the planet, to which these actors might contribute in ways I could only guess.

One metaphor for drama is that characters with fixed traits are placed in a cozy sandbox. It's up to the dramatist to figure out what the interactions will be, assuming an inevitability as would a chemist mixing chemicals. I for one do not think human interactions this inevitable, but after the fact one can see how certain outcomes were in the cards. Yes—sandbox, chemical solutions, cards—in one short paragraph I've mixed three metaphors. I never claimed to be a great writer.

So what happened that week in the House of Durrell? I'll remind you of my broken chain of romance, in case you can't keep it straight. Rebuffed by Albert, the polyamorous Melusina was now fixed on Jasmine, who, rebuffed by Darcy, had begun to reciprocate as an initiate to Lesbos. For his part, Darcy had a kid's crush on Gayle, who was drawn to me, poor Beasley. I simply didn't feel it for this all-American young woman and earnest environmentalist. But I also sensed that she felt a reluctance of her own, focusing on males she could count on for rejection. Why I didn't then know—read on.

No, I had been stirred instead by exotic Armide. I'd say right away that I felt the inappropriateness of my attentions, as someone three times her age and in no way a Muslim. As we drove up to the House of Durrell I addressed fatuities to her in her native Turkish. My knowledge of her language was my entrée as I gathered more of her bio and sought to ingratiate myself.

Armide Asani was a Sunni Muslim, born to a Turkish Cypriot couple, whose own parents had fled the Páphos area after the Turkish invasion, heading north to the village of Kythrea and a house then emptied of Greek Cypriots and assigned to them by the usurping Turkish authority. Under provisions of the recent reunification of the island, she and three siblings returned to the very house in the southwest village of Akoúrsos that the Asani family had previously occupied. Here she found on her iPhone the ad for human subjects in a nearby experiment sponsored by the Soros foundation.

At the University of Cyprus, Nicosia, Armide was studying podiatry because Cypriots are always twisting ankles and breaking toes on the brutally cobbled alleyways. Though in love with cars, Cypriots must grudgingly travel by foot wherever cars cannot reach. In Cyprus there is as much need for podiatrists as there is in Japan for oncologists specializing in lung cancer. School was now out of session, so she could tag along with think-tank members in efforts to save her island. Despite her pursuit of a science, Armide declined the modern secularization of Muslim women in Cyprus and elsewhere, wore traditional garb, and read the Qur'an devotionally. If she were in the company of an interested young man, she would always be accompanied by two protective brothers. At twenty-one she was ripe for the marriage market, had maintained her virginity, had been spared the sight of an adult penis, but was still possessed of a certain worldly insight and humor in matters romantic.

Armide remarked that, after recent injections by Albert during sessions with Renaud, she had begun feeling a strange new sensitivity to others, including total strangers. I surmised that empathy isn't necessarily moral but is sometimes merely sensate. If she saw somebody scratching an itch in his ribcage, she would feel the same itch and need to scratch. If she saw a shoplifter cop a pomegranate, she felt compelled to follow suit, though she had few skills as a larcenist and didn't even like pomegranates.

When the three impersonators arrived, Armide told me that she felt a deep world-weariness at the very sight of Lawrence Durrell, which gave away to boyish buoyancy at the sight of Gerald, which reverted in microseconds to a disordering of all her senses at the very sight of Arthur Rimbaud. There is, I know, a term for this— mirror-touch synesthesia, an abundance of empathy that might be regarded not as moral virtue but as painful pathology. Was this the result of Albert's injections? Stay tuned.

We all gathered in the living room. "This is where I beheld a heifer chewing cud the first day I visited the house," said Lawrence Durrell wearily. "The previous owner stored his animals here." We already knew this story and felt like yawning.

"You're probably wondering how we should spend our time while we're here," I said, "and I have a proposal."

Melusina was only half joking when she interjected, "Group sex!"

Lawrence perked up at this, while Arthur clutched his stomach.

"Thanks, Melusina, but no thanks. Group sex would be unseemly for a think tank." I then proposed that our three impersonators perform an improvisational skit on the balcony as the first of many theatricals.

Arthur interrupted. "But Monsieur Beasley, we are *not* impersonators! We *are* Arthur Rimbaud, Gerald Durrell, and Lawrence Durrell. *Vraiment.* This is not acting. Why cannot you get this through your thick Canadian skull? We are for *real!*" Rimbaud glared at me with his fiery blue eyes. There was the hint of a cruel smile.

"Yes," cried Gerald. "I'm one hundred percent me and Larry here is the real animal in my family."

"Okay, understood. But let's get down to business. The rain is letting up, so we can use the balcony as a stage." All of a sudden I thought to break the diplomatic decorum that normally defines me. "Let me be frank. Arthur and Larry, you haven't done well with your biographers. They dwell on sadism in your treatment of others. Gerry, you come off a little better, being kind to animals, but you're cruel about your sister's acne. And Larry, your promiscuity is legend, though how someone so diminutive could find willing partners is a puzzle. Your daughter Sappho told her analyst that you molested her, and then she killed herself. Beneath your urbanity and ability as a writer is a ferocity just barely held in check. So all of you, the play's the thing in which to catch your conscience and hope for better treatment by your biographers."

I was being an opportunist, deliberately baiting them, sensing they might be more dramatic if pissed off, and more likely to give me good material. Arthur, Lawrence, and Gerald eyed me discourteously while I pondered plot possibilities.

"At my suggestion, the Soros foundation has purchased this manor to serve as a cultural center for Northern Cyprus, with a theater, an art gallery, an internet café. Also a small press specializing in naive nature poetry and artless short fiction by locals."

In a corner Rimbaud looked down at his long dirty fingernails and appeared sullen. Maybe following my lead, Lawrence Durrell had it out for him. "Rimbaud, I've been meaning to ask this all my life. You let down the world of letters, trading in your prodigious talent for a life of human trafficking, gunrunning, and buggery. How could you prefer bossing a construction crew on this wretched island to writing 'Bateau ivre' and *The Illuminations*? You inspired my friend Henry Miller's *The Time of the Assassins*, granted it was his worst book ever."

Rimbaud had a ready answer as he whipped out his dagger. "Haven't you read Enid Starkie's biography? I've not read it myself because I was long dead when it appeared in 1947 and rely on what I've heard of it in hell. She had the answer. Having aspired to the bright sun of literary achievement, I saw that I was instead a fallen angel, a grubby little Satan who offended the sun god. I thought it best to save my soul by turning heels on the whole enterprise. Gunrunning, buggery, and slaving are nothing next to the inebriated prideful scribblings of my late teens. I renounced that crap and set out for a life without meaning or purpose beyond making money and escaping my mother."

Lawrence Durrell rubbed his pug nose, grinned, and seemed satisfied with this. "You have a point, Rimbaud. Maybe I should have packed it in after my *Quartet*. That's when I was a seer like you. Critics say I dwindled with my new fame and had used up my best material. I resorted to writing coffee-table books about islands. Enough said. Say, would you mind putting away that dagger?"

"Bart, somebody you have promised isn't showing up yet!" complained Melusina.

"Oh, you mean Shakespeare. Probably lost his way ... doesn't know where Cyprus is any more than Bohemia. He'll be here, carrying cheap quartos of *Othello* and his sonnets. Thing is, I'm not sure he'll be of much use. I'm trying right now to think up a plot for our improv team, but Shakespeare came up empty with plots, had to pilfer them on the run. Still, he'll be a good addition. He's great at singing incomprehensible lyrics and obscene ditties. We can cast him in our improvs but not the starring roles." I turned around. "Do you hear a knocking at the gate?"

In her swirling toga, Melusina ran to answer it, shouting through the door that nobody had been murdered yet and she wasn't drunk. Do you catch this? She was making a learned application of *Macbeth*'s drunken porter scene. She opened the door and there stood William Shakespeare, the exact replica of his visage in the First Folio of 1623, a huge head with receding hairline but long locks to left and right, starched ruff, and tight doublet with broad shoulders. Below he sported wide trunks tied at the knee, silken hose, embroidered gloves, old buskins decorated with fake roses, a modest codpiece, and at his belt, a dagger, the second now in our company. He appeared to be in his mid to late forties. His forehead was bulbous. As my compatriot critic Northrop Frye once said of the 1623 Droeshout engraving, Shakespeare "looks like an idiot."

"*Jawohl*, you are the Shakespeare impersonator," Melusina announced.

"Impersonator? Thou fragment! *I am Shakespeare* summoned here by the Crown." Shakespeare leapt four feet into the air and whirled about, confronting Melusina who tilted backward. "Why is nobody yet murthered? Pray, what is the argument of this play? . . . Betimes, I come to seize your berry, not to praise it."

Holding his paunch with guffaws not unlike an unseemly dramatic portrayal of Mozart in 1979, Shakespeare found his witticism more amusing than we did, but our skin was still crawling because it seemed the Bard had from the dead awakened. Even Rimbaud was terrified and fell to the floor in abject quivering and snorting. Though I had engineered this spectral resuscitation, I was tempted to run upstairs and leap from the balcony.

Shakespeare stooped and hoisted limp Rimbaud over his shoulders. "Has his highness fallen into a whoreson apoplexy? A cup of sack with lime for this villainous coward." With no sack in the House of Durrell, Jasmine ran to the larder for a cup of zivanía and administered it to the Frenchman, who came to but was flung back hard on the floor by the Bard, who brandished his dagger.

I thought of how this had all come about—my dissatisfaction with my prosaic dreamworld, my need for words—and despite the dagger, vowed to push onward with the central question that had always dogged Shakespeare studies.

"Will—if I may presume—did you write your plays or should somebody else be getting the credit?"

He waved the dagger. "Certes, you decide, witling. Scrivener's palsy is proof palpable of my labors. Look, what I speak, my life shall prove it true. But alas, to make me a fixed figure for the time of scorn to point his slow unmoving finger at! Oh, when degree is shaked, which is the ladder to all high designs, the enterprise is sick! Take but degree away, untune that string, and hark, what discord follows! Then everything includes itself in power, power into will, will into appetite, and appetite, a universal wolf, so doubly seconded with will and power, must make perforce a universal prey, and last eat up himself . . . Got that?"

Shakespeare bit on his right arm to underscore his metaphor. Clearly he wished to command the Great Chain of Being. From time to time he whirled about like a villain in a nineteenth-century stage melodrama. Then he made the rounds, strutting up to each of us. We took turns stepping back in dread.

"Pray, let copulation thrive. Dost thou think because thou art virtuous, there shall be no more cakes and ale?"

Rimbaud replied meekly that he was all for having a party.

Now that the Bard was here, I suggested we improvise a play to be performed on the balcony just for fun. "Will, would you have a plot up your sleeve?"

"What meaning lieth here? If I conceive you, yes, I purloined one from a Roman coxcomb for *Love's Labour's Won*."

"Hmmm, that's the one play of yours apparently lost for all time. Do you recall the plot?"

"By my troth but hoist *Love's Labour's Lost* to a glass."

"Oh, you mean to a mirror, as in *Alice Through the Looking-Glass*?"

"Who? What?"

"Oh, right, you don't know any works of literature after 1616. Ever hear of John Milton or Mickey Spillane?"

"Who?"

"Or Hitler?"

"Who?"

"He wrote a well-known book, but never mind."

"Inquire after *Ralph Roister Doister* or *Gammer Gurton's Needle*, for they are dukedom large enough. Now thou flap-mouthed rascal, pertaining to a plot—someone in this foyer is murthered and we uncover who the culprit be. Such a culprit there was in my *Richard the Third* or perchance 'twas *the Second*, no matter."

I found this startling. "Will, you aren't suggesting that one of us should be *murthered*? Seems excessive for a parlor game."

"Very well then, let me ponder further what the play shall be." He scratched at his bulbous forehead. "Might you have at hand a folio of *Holinshed's Chronicles*—this hath provisioned forth many a plot when watersnipes at the Globe solicited a play of me in less than a fortnight. Ingrates! At the last I lit fire to the theater and returned in haste to mine own Stratford-on-Avon. There I beguiled the hours suing a neighbor to recover six pounds and beheld my daughter Judith marry poorly. Then, deciding not to be, I made my quietus with poison, the Muse having departed five years earlier. This was the salubrious exit of the lean unwashed artificer who wearied of writing those plays, brought forth in trifling quartos unlike the elegant folio in which my scurrilous compeer Ben Jonson—a murtherer, by the way— found his immortality well before the grave oped even for him. But I carry one here, entitled *Othello*, a quarto that containeth words of my coinage."

Shakespeare then turned and muttered to an empty wall, again scratching at his forehead, gesticulating angrily to unseen observers, and swirling around to take stock of the available actors, all of us surely out of Central Casting and unworthy.

"Okay, Will, calm down. I'll take over." I turned to the others. "I suggest we improvise on this very play *Othello*—loosely, of course. We have only one copy and it's a little solemn for a parlor game. But an appropriate choice. Acts two through five are set in Cyprus, described by you as a 'warlike isle.'"

"All I ken about Cyprus deriveth from Giraldi Cinthio's *Hecatommithi*," said Shakespeare. "And that glass-gazing, superserviceable, finical rogue Ben Jonson said I lacked learning! I read it in the Italian... Problem was I didn't know Italian and leaned on Latinate cognates... Problem was I had small Latin."

"Still, Will, you penned an astonishing play, a monument in the Western canon."

"There are blemishes I might have remedied, for Cassio is both married and unmarried. But I never blotted a line."

"It's a great tragedy and will survive the travesty I'm now proposing. I'll take over the casting. Arthur Rimbaud, it's obvious you should play Iago. You're totally devoid of conscience."

Rimbaud nodded and smirked, again brandishing his dagger that made everybody except Shakespeare, also possessed of a dagger, cringe and back away. "*Grand merci*, Monsieur Beasley, I'll be happy to slay the cast. Where do I begin?"

"Let me think this through, Arthur." I paused and thought it through. Casting a play sets the initial conditions from which all else flows, and I wished to get it right, even though this was meant to be no more serious than bingo. "Okay, remember this is just for fun—nobody gets killed. Everybody laughs because we'll imitate mankind so abominably, to echo the Bard's language. The role of Othello goes to Lawrence Durrell." Muted applause. "As has been made plain by your biographers, Larry, you frequently became unhinged by jealousy and treated your wife Eve with great cruelty, even while your friends saw you as generous and gregarious. Othello is a good fit."

Melusina interrupted. "I am Desdemona. I am being blonde and to starring roles am accustomed."

"Sorry," I replied. "Your morals don't fit. Polyamory is not in Desdemona's repertoire. No, Melusina Frei, you'll be playing Bianca the courtesan. A small role as Cassio's squeeze, but you can expand it as you like. Gayle Drake-Larkin, you'll be playing Desdemona."

Melusina frowned, while everybody else not holding a dagger applauded. "Desdemona is allowed by the 'enchafèd flood' to arrive safely in Cyprus," I continued, "like your luck, Gayle, in flying through thick and thin. And no hint of scandal has emerged from your work with Al Gore. You're not without a flirtatious streak but neither was Desdemona, to judge by act two, scene one, where she catches on to all the filthy innuendos."

I couldn't help but notice the lewd slitted eyes that Lawrence Durrell turned toward Armide, as if already making the beast with two backs. Gayle said, "I'll play Desdemona, but let's not let this parlor game get out of hand. Please, no pillow!"

"Jasmine Ivory, you'll play Emilia, attendant to Desdemona and unfortunate wife of Iago—a realist whose speech closing act four is a landmark in the history of feminism. You'll also be outing Iago for the villain he is."

"Feminism, of what speakest thou?" asked Shakespeare.

I peered at him. "You'll be getting a bad rap for willing your wife that second-best bed. Is it too late to change your will, Will?"

"I have my reasons."

"The role of Cassio goes to Darcy Peatman. He is Othello's trusted lieutenant, honorable but given to braggadocio when he's elevated in rank above Iago. Like you Darcy, Cassio is a cheap drunk. And there's no evidence that he is not a vegetarian or that he is unkind to animals."

"Fine by me. Nobody can play the role of Cassio better than I. Nobody!"

"Okay, settle down, Darcy." Considering that two of our company had daggers and that nobody in the House of Durrell was totally sane, I felt the casting was going fairly well. "Now the role of Roderigo goes to Gerald Durrell. He's the gull Iago persuades has a chance for the hand of Desdemona. Gerry, you are the youngster in the Durrell family and know what it's like to be immature and impulsive. Granted you are more turned on by grackles than girls. But *gull* is also the name of an aquatic bird. So the role is a good fit."

"Many thanks, Bart. As I recall, Roderigo wises up too late to avoid being scuttled by Iago. Thank you in advance, Arthur. Just remember, no real daggers. I'll play the part for laughs."

I then addressed our Turkish Cypriot in Turkish. "Because your English is rudimentary, I'll ask you, Armide Asani, to be the understudy to Gayle's Desdemona. All you need do is follow her around and make some sound effects and serve as prop girl. We'll use dinner forks as swords and edit out the pillow but keep the handkerchief."

I communicated this to the others also, who nodded. I took some pleasure in then telling the Bard what his role would be.

"As you for you, William Shakespeare, either you or Edward de Vere wrote this play, and though you often played roles at the Globe, I'll ask you to serve instead as dramaturg. Stand aside, Will, and comment on whether the players are faithfully representing your intentions, making allowance for improvisation and the conversion of your great tragedy into asinine farce."

Shakespeare demurred. "I confess to having no intentions. What meanest thou, *intentions*?"

"That's why you're a universal blank and open target for deluded critics. You've disappeared behind your plays. I won't play a part either but I'll direct and stage manage. Now, in the spirit of act two, scene three, let us ope the larder, stuff ourselves, and get drunk. Then, ho! To the balcony we shall go!"

Chapter Twelve

THE PLAY'S THE THING

Jasmine took charge of opening the larder and setting out goblets brimming with zivanía. This proved ill-advised.

"Act two, scene two is a drunken brawl, eh, Will?" I asked.

"Forsooth, I do not recall," he replied, thumbing awkwardly through his quarto. "Soft, let me inquiry make."

"Iago gets Cassio drunk," I explained, "and has set up Roderigo to insult him. A duel follows. Cassio takes the rap and is cast out of Othello's favor. Does this ring a bell, Will?"

"What meanest thou, 'ring a bell'? But no matter, let us forthwith invade the larder."

The party of ten wasted no time in feasting on victuals and beverages provided by the Soros foundation, which, as you've gathered, is the Unmoved Mover throughout this narrative. Armide focused on Turkish delicacies—*karniyarik*, *karagöz*, and *salyangoz*, with *katmer* for dessert, lifting her niqab to shovel them in. You already know these dishes from the Turkish Kitchen on the East Side. I imagined the lucky edibles making their way down her gullet. But frankly I had no intention of seducing her, old enough to be her great grandfather. In earlier days, I relied on sweet talk and seductive body language, with mixed results. If I relied on body language today, I'd have no results. At five foot seven, I'm now two inches shorter than in my MIT days, have lost much of my thick auburn hair, and have a double chin unless I prop my head up, yellowed teeth, and minimal musculature from a lifelong aversion to working out. Still, I'm said to have an amiable mug, and there's that calming Canadian disposition for which everybody north of the border is irritatingly praised.

As I stood by, Lawrence Durrell, who also spoke perfect Turkish, played his hand. "Armide, you may be the mere understudy to my wife, Desdemona, but you are still my wife, just once removed. Would you care to share some of that *katmer*?"

"Sure, Mister Durrell. I'm a devotee of *The Alexandria Quartet*, translated into Turkish. Do I, like, remind you of Justine?"

With Durrell's reputation as an improbably successful satyr in mind, I tried my best to stir up a dram within of the yellow bile. Nothing on my part was required because, sensing Durrell was making a move, Shakespeare himself intervened.

"This is off script and goatish, Othello. Eftsoons, lay off the virtuous Armide."

"Nobody follows your scripts anymore, Will," replied Lawrence Durrell. "The celebrated BBC production starring Ian McKellen edits out many of your better lines. In response to Desdemona's adultery with Cassio, Othello is supposed to say, 'It is the very error of the moon . . . She comes more nearer earth than she was wont . . . And makes men mad.' If these lines can be *cut*, surely we can *add* our own. You've discharged your commission, Will. Now step aside!"

Switching back to Turkish, Durrell continued his courtship of Armide, whose hips swayed enticingly. Shakespeare sighed at the futility of his intervention, then again thumbed his quarto.

Rimbaud replied, "Will, I am fully in accord with Monsieur Durrell and shall be adding my own excrementitious lines."

"All I ken about you, Monsieur Rimbaud, is what I have just ascertained from Master Durrell, since I was entombed two hundred and seventy-five years before you."

"Voilà! I was writing masterworks at the age of fifteen: 'Ophélie,' *par example*, based on your *Hamlet*. You didn't pen that play until thirty-six, just one year before I died, and as for *Richard the Third*, your first play of any merit, you were already twenty-eight, *presque* twice my age. *J'étais l'enfant prodige.* You worked hard at your craft."

Leaving off his seduction of Armide, Lawrence Durrell observed, "My early memoir *Prospero's Cell* leans heavily on your *Tempest*, Will. And drowning one's book is a strong temptation for any serious writer. As for you, Arthur, you wrote some lines that aren't at all bad for a teenager. '*Sûr l'onde calme et noire où dorment étoiles... La blanche Ophélia flotte comme un grand lys...*' Translated for anyone here ignorant of French—'On water calm and black where stars are sleeping... The white Ophelia floats like a wondrous lily.' Will, the lad has a point. Many youngsters from the Midwest in the sixties were greater enthusiasts of my *Quartet* than your plays. It was easier to identify with Justine than with Cleopatra. She was long in the tooth, and your way of putting things wasn't cool. This is in no way to diminish your great achievement."

Gerald Durrell reminded us that the parlor game was to be a farcical enactment of *Othello*, not an exercise in self-promotion. But he joined in the competitive chatter with some telling analogies. "Will, you remind me of the betsileo sportive lemur because of your legendary ability to leap from tree to tree. Arthur, you put me in mind of an Ethiopian African mole rat who should return to its burrow where it belongs, the sooner the better. And Larry, you resemble my brother, Larry, who is much like a Natal Midlands dwarf chameleon with a long sticky tongue adapted for catching flies. And I remind myself of a grey-rumped treeswift, for reasons I do not fully grasp."

Holding his gerbil, Gerald Durrell was obliquely alluding to the various flirtations and gambits that were underway in the House of Durrell. It was easy to see, now that feasting and drinking had done their worst, that the four impersonators had selected targets from among the think-tank fellows and our token Muslim. Lawrence Durrell was again cornering Armide, while I looked on disapprovingly. William Shakespeare was ogling Jasmine, to the obvious displeasure of Melusina, less polyamorous by the minute. Gerald Durrell was onto Gayle, which vexed Darcy, upstaged by his own idol. And Arthur Rimbaud was leering at me. Gayle didn't like this, nor did I.

If jealousy is at the center of *Othello*, we weren't so far off script. All this was taking place in a lurid courtship dance within alcoves, boudoirs, and hallways.

Some conversations I overheard. Since Muslim women the world over had only a year earlier declared their sexual independence, Lawrence Durrell had reason to hope his flatteries would as usual prevail. In Turkish: "I see you through multiple mirrors, Armide. The many-sided prism of your inner complexity— within the realm of what I term the *heraldic universe*, a vast symbol system wherein sex plays the central role. Let us share this moment and become part owners one of the other in the explosive violence of our shared passion."

Armide lifted her niqad, scowled, and replied with the Turkish equivalent of Joyce's line in *Dubliners*, "Like, 'men that is now is only all palaver and what they can get out of you.'" She pushed Lawrence Durrell's stubby hand aside and, a few inches taller, looked down at the little fellow with contempt. "I read *The Alexandria Quartet* and fell in love with its author—until I just now met the author. I would have thought you, like, more comely and world-weary, and not so ready to quote yourself in an uncool come-on. Mister Durrell, like, take a walk!"

"At the least, Armide," I said in my best Turkish, "let's remember that without this author, there would be no House of Durrell where feasting and acting can take place. Let's give him that much. Can we step out to the balcony?"

Not really wishing to win Armide for myself, I was gallant enough to protect her from Lawrence Durrell. He resisted. "If you interfere, Bart, I'll see to it that your next memoir is panned in the *Observer*."

As we stood there muttering inanities, I imagined a fleeting dark shadow at the latticed front casement. This I attributed to the fabled zivanía, known to produce hallucinations. But sober Armide too glanced over at the casement and shivered.

It came to mind that I'm Canadian and that Lawrence Durrell was an unrepentant Royalist. "Perhaps we should—as subjects of her majesty—both step aside and let the lady choose, my dear Larry. All I can offer Armide is a warm curiosity and refined manners, not a heraldic universe, whatever the devil that is. Also, I'm three inches taller and not at all dead." Durrell shrugged his shoulders and sighed, knowing what I'd said was unanswerable.

"Okay, boys, you've given me enough to work on," said Armide. "I'll eat up more *karniyarik* and, like, think it over. Meanwhile, mirror-touch synesthesia is telling me that both you jerks are total frauds!"

I left the two of them and crossed over to the southwest alcove where Shakespeare was chatting up Jasmine with wide-eyed Melusina looking on, ready for an intervention of her own. "Might I quote myself, fair Jasmina?" He pulled out the quarto of his sonnets and fumbled with pages. Finally, "'In old age, black was not counted fair ... Or, if it were, it bore not beauty's name ... But now is black beauty's successive heir ...' Would'st thou protest mine Dark Lady to be?"

"I'll consider it, Will, but rumor has it that you're enamored of a fair youth you oddly encourage to propagate, to the extent he considers you totally bonkers."

"Alack, albeit the world's greatest bard I confess to strange appetites. He calleth himself Willie Hughes, a musician who hath just learned to shave. It pleaseth me to defuse this errant passion and indite the remaining twenty-five sonnets to you."

"Master Shakespeare," said Melusina with irritation, "I am cast as the courtesan Bianca in your tragedy, and *ja*, Jasmine here is having the greater role as Emilia. But she and I are to the end of time in Sapphic bliss united." She paused and looked at Jasmine quizzically. Silence, and then more silence. "Though, a ménage à trois is not being out of the question. There's an empty boudoir upstairs. What are you thinking, Jasmine? Will is being very cute in that starched ruff."

Alas, Melusina was relapsing into polyamory. Maybe we pardon her in this circumstance?

"Fine, but just this once," said Jasmine. "I can always say I got it on with the immortal Shakespeare, no matter what happens."

"I shall no promises make and am oft by nausea overcome, but lead on."

I stepped aside as the three made their way up the stairs, with unseemly giggles. The moral of this farce is that reality theater doesn't well conform to canonical masterworks.

Gerald Durrell had his own way of eliciting the interest of a potential mate, based on antics of animal courtship. Darcy must have wondered how Gayle would respond to his own role model as a competitor in romance.

"Have you seen the greater flamingoes in the Great Salt Lake near the Hala Sultan Tekke?" asked Gerald.

"Yes," replied Gayle, "I flew over them in a retrofitted Cessna and our computer Agie counted them—31,415, as I recall."

"Great moralists, those flamingoes. There may have been 31,415 of them and to your eyes they all looked alike, but they go through elaborate rituals and mate for life. 'Don't even think of messing around with Fluella,' says one flamingo to another. 'She's my bird!'"

"I like birds because they remind me of planes," said Gayle, "or maybe it's the other way around. Either way, I fly like a bird."

"If you don't mind, I'll show you how the male greater flamingo goes about attracting a mate."

"I think *I* mind," said Darcy, anxiously watching Gayle warm to the Gerald Durrell impersonator.

"Oh go away, Darcy," said Gayle. "I wanna see it. Remember, Bart said Roderigo should make a fool of himself. Go ahead, Gerry, show me."

Still holding his gerbil, Gerald Durrell stood on one leg, impressive given the drops of zivanía he'd taken. He stretched his neck, jerked his head from side to side, flapped his arms while clutching the gerbil, and from his turned-up bill emitted a loud nasal *ar-honk, ar-honk, ar-honk* that brought the naked ménage to their chamber door upstairs. A pair of mating dragonflies landed on the head of his gerbil and went about their business.

Gayle was charmed by the brilliant mimicry and asked Gerald to do it all over again. Darcy then lost the "daily beauty" of his assigned role of Cassio. "I can do that too!" he shouted as he tried to stand on one leg, promptly losing balance and falling over backward. "Oh bloody shit!"

Gayle couldn't help laughing.

Gerald pressed his advantage but Gayle as usual played hard to get. "No kissing just now, Gerry," she said, looking my way to signal that I, and neither Darcy nor Gerald, remained her principal romantic interest. "Let's get us more *seftalies*."

It was then that Rimbaud, my Iago, approached me with his paralyzing blue eyes and whispered, "I like not that. Did you see Armide just now? Monsieur Lawrence Durrell gave her a spoonful of *katmer* and the two repaired to the balcony. Look to her, Canadian, but beware the green-eyed monster, *la jalousie*."

"Arthur, your Iago impersonation is even better than your Arthur Rimbaud impersonation. But know my infatuation with Armide is as mild as it is hopeless—hopeless because she would always give her heart to a best-selling superstar, even a dead one, over a midlist author like me."

Rimbaud paused and relit his pipe, seeming to take this in. He changed the subject. "I left this wretched island after supervising construction of the governor's hunting lodge. I knew *rien du tout* about construction."

"Yes, you then briefly served as clerk at the Cave of the Virgin Troödhitissa after whacking one of your workers and running away."

"*Bien sûr*, it was—"

"Do you recall leaving a notebook behind?"

"*Oui! Celui-là* contained my best work since *Illuminations*—my *only* work for I had resumed writing *pour un moment* during my first stay in Cyprus. How know you this?"

"I found it some one hundred and thirty years after your death and will have it auctioned at Sotheby's—a good test of your standing within the literary community."

"But I want it back *immédiatement!*"

"Sure thing. Go tell a clerk at Sotheby's that you are Arthur Rimbaud and the notebook is yours alone to sell!"

Art was reaching for his dagger when there was a scream and fracas on the balcony. This was for me a fortunate diversion for I feared that Rimbaud would either stab me or make a pass, and my own sexuality is totally conventional. There's no way I'd ever agree to have sex with Arthur Rimbaud. I was also relieved because this tomfoolery had gone on long enough and, like you readers, I wished for a change of pace. We all dropped what we were doing—including the group-sex nonsense—and ran up the staircase to the balcony.

There we beheld Lawrence Durrell tied up with a handkerchief in his mouth. An important prop in *Othello* but serving a different purpose here. Armide was nowhere in sight.

"Okay, everybody," I said, "now we know the plot of our play. The central action is the disappearance of Armide and the dénouement will be her recovery. Let's not panic."

I panicked. Where was she? I headed up the search, overriding the great Shakespeare, who was never forthcoming in stage directions. "Exit stage left, Will. Darcy, open all interior trapdoors. Gayle, take hold of that rigging, fly around, and try to spot Armide and her abductor offstage. Jasmine, look in the larder downstage, just in case."

The author of *The Alexandria Quartet*—a smallish pile of pug-nosed humanity tied hand to feet, squirming impatiently and emitting muffled protestations—staggered upright as soon as we pulled the handkerchief from out his mouth and freed up his drunken limbs. He appeared more chagrined than terrified. Who was his assailant, we asked, and where was Armide?

"Kidnapped!" Lawrence Durrell replied. "The scoundrel was an unscrubbed Greek Cypriot in his early twenties. She called him *Renaud*. He called me an Anglo-Indian scumbag and said I should lay off seducing his girl. Because she spoke little Greek and he no Turkish, I offered at knifepoint to serve as interpreter. She said he had no entitlement, also something about their participation in a double-blind experiment—had to dig deep into my Greek word-hoard for *double-blind*. He grabbed at her and she screamed, calling him a damned heathen as he tied me up with one hand and held her by the niqab with the other. Skillful, must say. Happily, he forgot to slit my throat, and I heard a moped spin off. My gratitude for rescuing me, especially you, Gerry. You have few kind words for me in *My Family and Other Animals*. By the way, I cannot help but notice that some of you are naked. Am I a party pooper? Will, you are in remarkably good shape for somebody more than four centuries old."

Flattered, Shakespeare replied that he modeled himself on Charles the wrestler in *As You Like It*.

"But Will, Charles is defeated, thrown to the ground by Orlando," noted Lawrence Durrell.

"Drat! Well then, I imitate Orlando."

Darcy interrupted. "You all prattle on to no purpose. As the virtuous Cassio I must ask, What the fickin' fuck are we to do?"

"We chase after them," I said. "Come on, think tank, and you too, Shakespeare, Rimbaud, and Durrell brothers. Let's pack into the Rover—you know, the unclobbered one."

Speaking for the other impersonators, Rimbaud begged off, and not because it would be too much like that absurd collegiate sport of packing a Volkswagen. "*C'est dommage.* We signed on with the

Soros foundation for a theatrical entertainment *seulement* and not—*comment dirai-je?*—some wild goose chase. We have engagements elsewhere as much sought after professionals. There's *beaucoup* I must do before I die of bone cancer at the age of thirty-seven."

William Shakespeare, Lawrence Durrell, and Gerald Durrell nodded. This is the ingrained narcissism of great writers. They cannot be counted on for heroic deeds beyond the writing desk. Writing is the writer's action. Biographies of writers must dwell on everything in a writer's life except the main thing, the act of sitting at that desk.

"If she is rescued, do give Armide my warmest praise for her attentions—sorry Bart," said Lawrence Durrell. "Also for the esteem in which he holds my *Quartet*. Tell her to put my *Avignon Quintet* on her bucket list, available cheap on Amazon."

Bucket list? I thought Durrell had perished well before this unfortunate phrase became a staple of popular culture.

Gerald Durrell chimed in. "My brother is rather full of himself. He writes for love of writing, I for need of money—to subsidize my zoo. Tell Armide that if she survives, she might consider giving to the Durrell Wildlife Conservation Trust, where I'm trying to clone a dodo."

William Shakespeare chimed in, "Yes, I am much aggrieved to depart like this, but farewell, thou art too dear for my possessing, Melusina and Jasmina. Armida is nowhere to be found in my dramatis personae but she was well cast as understudy to the fair Desdemona. Her scream upon abduction betrays a player's promise. And now, zounds, I must take my leave. Anne hath been asking too many questions in her damned textings."

The four impersonators packed up their stuff and disappeared into the night.

Chapter Thirteen

GAYLE'S STORY

In earlier times the great storm would have knocked out all communications, but in 2024 cell phones still worked despite the grid's collapse. Gayle called the pan-Cypriot police and Reuters with word of the kidnapping. "Look out for a Greek Cypriot male desperado answering to the name of Renaud and a screaming Turkish Cypriot female virgin who answers to Armide. He's holding her captive on a moped. We fear for her life."

She also put in a call to Albert, back in Dhroúsha monitoring his human subjects. He'd been loath to give Armide permission to depart for the North, and doing so gave Renaud a temporary out from the double-blind experiment. "Albert," said Gayle, "you know the couple. Bring your lab notes and some syringes of the real Empathomax."

"*Feh!*" I overheard Albert reply. "I can't leave my goddam guinea pigs any more than a Nobel geneticist can leave his fruit flies. Kudos on solving the desertification problem and meeting up with Shakespeare, Charles Rimbaud, and the Burrough brothers. But desertification isn't my issue and I don't give a hoot about literature."

"Aren't Armide and Renaud vital guinea pigs? They'll get you the data you need," Gayle replied.

Melusina got on the cell and threatened to betray some secrets to the other fellows about Albert's personal habits she'd observed at the Chelidonia if he didn't oblige. What these were I didn't know or wish to. Albert grumbled and demurred. I overheard him mutter, "*Nem zich a vaneh*," go jump in the lake. But he agreed to call the Poseidon Taxi Service and asked where he should meet us.

We paused. Come to think of it, where might we pick up the trail? The Cypriot police were renowned for being loafers ever since reunification, and Reuters got everything wrong when it came to Cyprus. It was up to us to rescue Armide.

Melusina was the clairvoyant of the think tank. She had directly intuited the underwater Aphrodite, and her welkin eyes suggested powers of a seer. Counting Rimbaud, you readers have two welkin-eyed seers in one Kindle download.

"I'm getting a strong tug in the direction of the Museum of Liberation Struggle in Nicosia—*wissen sie*, the world's most grisly collection of war memorabilia. I am thinking they check into the Cleopatra Hotel, in the near of there. Albert, meet us now at the Cleopatra Hotel in Nicosia . . . No, that's an order!" A grunt on the other end signaled consent.

We were impressed by how specific Melusina's intuition was. To be sure, there was no evidence that the two were *not* checking into the Cleopatra Hotel. A call to the hotel was unproductive because the clerks were forbidden to divulge information about guests. Theirs was a hotel best known for assignations. Melusina explained to us that it wasn't clairvoyance alone but reasonable inference. It made sense that the Greek Cypriot Renaud, if smitten with Armide, would try to reeducate this Turkish Cypriot. The Museum of Liberation Struggle was the place to begin. Lots of photographic documentation of the Greek Cypriots' struggle against the Brits. "Renaud would show Armide how Greek Cypriots like himself have been heroic in bumping off Brits," said Melusina. "But the curators edit out how they also bumped off lots of Turkish Cypriots. Take it from an archeologist, kids are not understanding history and never will. Curators are not either."

With Gayle again at the wheel, we five departed in the Rover but were promptly trapped between two mudslides three miles apart on the road to Famagusta. We sat in the automobile for two days while Cypriot road crews took many breaks. Jasmine had packed two iced picnic baskets and zivanía, so we ate, drank, chatted, discreetly left the car when bushes were called for, and spent some time better acquainting ourselves one with another.

Darcy expressed disappointment with Gerald Durrell. "What a clown and not even a vegetarian! And a lousy Roderigo." We all knew that Gerald had made a play for Gayle, so Darcy was hardly without bias.

For her part Melusina expressed disappointment with Shakespeare. "He was looking ridiculous in that tunic and has not known much about his own plays. Willing to go with the ménage but Armide has shrieked just as Jasmine and I the moldy codpiece were negotiating, so neither Jasmine nor I can claim to be making it to the hilltop with the Bard." Of course Melusina, possessive of Jasmine, could hardly be objective.

I confessed disappointment with Lawrence Durrell for the usual reasons. "He just didn't look the part of the world-weary Darley. His vocabulary was no better than my own and the narcissism was offensive." I couldn't be wholly impartial since he'd seemed to be winning the attentions of Armide, a slight blow to my vanity if in no way the occasion for jealousy. I dared not express disappointment with Rimbaud for fear of political incorrectness as a cis-male, who shouldn't take offense at a gay overture. But Melusina, Jasmine, and Gayle all said that he was a real creep.

Better not to meet the greats, I reflected. Do we truly wish to have dinner with Homer, Beethoven, Einstein, and Lady Gaga? Let us be content to know them through the towering works.

Passing the zivanía and chomping down on the *gourounópoulo*— suckling pig—except Darcy, who was partial to the *kappari*— pickled caper plants—we got more personal. Having read my narrative this far, you may ask that I further develop these characters, discover their underbellies, so you might *care* for them. My agent always insists he must be "passionate" about my characters or he will drop me for not answering to his inherently passionate nature. Tennessee Williams understood this well, giving his characters a monologue of melodramatic self-revelation late in the day. "Oh God, here it comes!" The ticket holder sighs in resignation to the ordeal of deep explanation.

I was sitting in the front seat next to Gayle, who again squeezed my knee, this time the right. "Ouch!" At one in the morning, she was wholly drunk and the next day would remember little of what she had divulged. "Bart, you said I should take an interest in Darcy—that you were strictly unavailable." Darcy sighed and swallowed a caper. "Well, there's a reason for this, if you all must know. Yup, I'm an ardent environmentalist and worked hard for Al Gore. One of the few politicians who was unavailable, then at least. This is my story." I silently vowed to stay awake, owing her this much.

"My father was a tenure-track assistant professor of biology at the University of Portland. I admired him and his love of the sciences rubbed off. I was only twelve when he was denied tenure because he got the wrong kind of grant—an NIH instead of an NSF. He was crushed but not altogether fired—as an assistant clinical professor he could stay on and teach for low wages and didn't need to get grants and publish. It's just that research and publication were all he wanted in life. So one day at his office he took a forty-five and stuck it in his mouth, making quite a mess. My mother was a social worker and managed to raise my two siblings and me, but she never remarried. Few guys wanna step in and marry a grieving widow with three kids. When we were all grown up and out of the house, she followed suit, killed herself, but with carbon monoxide, I guess not wanting to make a mess."

"Gayle, this is so sad!" exclaimed Melusina. "I have had no idea and I am being the clairvoyant."

"I keep it to myself. And it doesn't get any better. I'd always been popular, regarded as good-looking by the boys, lots of dates and time spent in back seats, but as a good Episcopalian I didn't lose my virginity. Saving it for my dead dad, a psychoanalyst said. I took up flying at seventeen and always got a charge from the freedom of it, getting away from bad memories and lighting out for the territory. Felt guilty at using fossil fuel for kicks. I bought the environmental thing heart and soul. Worked hard to protect forests around Portland and prevent offshore drilling. I finally lost my virginity to a co-environmentalist working for big Al. We did it in a tree house one night, unprotected sex. I'd waited so long it hurt. But what really hurt is that he was HIV positive."

We all gasped.

"And so am I. A heavy price to pay for a single flop in the hay—uh, make that swing in the tree. A few months later I began to suffer aches and chills, so I confronted him. Jim apologized— like the W saying 'sorry about that' for the Iraqi invasion. He'd meant to put on a condom but got carried away. Didn't wanna tell me about his HIV for fear of rejection. Guys are horny, let's face it. So I put the make only on unavailable men or impotent men, better both. Don't wish to pass this bug along. Yup, I could insist on condoms but am too spooked to take any risks. I take my risks as a pilot and driver, you've noticed? It's sorta nuts but I feel I'm a lethal environmentalist. Ironic, right? We're all obsessed with natural ingredients and vitamin supplements, but I need the HIV cocktail every morning, and it's no margarita."

"So that's why you spend so long in the loo, luv," observed Darcy, proud of his powers of inference.

"And why I rejected your advances and have come on to Bart here, who is unavailable. Right, Bart?"

"Hard to say. No longer married but I've learned it's better for you and anybody else not to get mixed up with me. I'm a writer and a midlisted one at that. We're no fun, fret too much about our little books. Just think you should look elsewhere. By the way, I wouldn't be frightened of your HIV, Gayle. I'm enlightened. But so sorry to hear about this. It's unfair."

"No time to feel sorry for myself," she said, turning around and looking us all in the eyes. "I'm in too big a hurry to water this island, maybe with fewer mudslides."

We were all made somber by Gayle's story and slowly drifted off to sleep. It was getting on to 7:00 a.m. when we awakened and looked out the windows at the drenched landscape, just beginning to brighten but desolate as the moon. Gayle jarred my estimate of my powers of judgment, for I had taken her to be a bright-eyed innocent and hardly a potentially tragic figure.

Nobody was in the mood for more self-revelation when Darcy announced it was now his turn. "It's a long story. You'll need to pay attention."

"Too early in the morning, Darcy. Save your story for later," I said, speaking for everybody. "They've cleared the road up ahead. Let's drive on to Nicosia."

We arrived at the Cleopatra Hotel and met up with Albert, grumpy and taciturn, having been driven to the hotel by the same Poseidon driver who escorted Melusina to Káthikas, but in an ancient Studebaker instead of a Rolls. It looked as if Albert had been sleeping in his clothes. I passed a coin to the concierge and asked if a young unscrubbed Greek Cypriot male and a Turkish Cypriot female had arrived two days earlier on a moped.

"Yes," he replied in English, free to speak now that the scamps had come and gone. "She seemed quite flustered upon arrival but this morning was of much better cheer. They spent yesterday in the Liberation Museum and had dinner here last night to recover. She had replaced her niqab with short shorts. They were the first on the dance floor. He taught her some Greek dances. Had to interfere when he was dancing on a tabletop and flinging saucers at the wall while humming the theme from *Zorba the Greek*. I didn't care about the saucers, I stopped him because it was so trite!"

"Sounds as if our abductee has warmed to her abductor!" exclaimed Darcy. "We've put ourselves out for nothing. Bloody business!"

"Any idea which way they were heading?" I asked.

"Not sure, but they were singing something about Famagusta in both Greek and Turkish when they climbed back on the moped. Schubert, if I'm not mistaken. She locked arms around him as off they sped."

"I could have predicted this," groused Albert. "In recent sessions they stopped biting and spitting. I've always known they were getting Empathomax and not the placebo."

Upon leaving we ran into an anachronistic newspaper boy holding the *Pan-Cypriot Gazette*. On the front page of this vestige of print culture was news in Greek of the abduction, complete with surveillance photos of the two picking up petrol at a garage outside Nicosia. *Investigators entered the laboratory of neurologist Albert Vygotsky in Dhroúsha and confiscated footage of the two taken during his experimental sessions. He is said to be enhancing "mirror neurons" that might achieve on the level of brain chemistry what decades of warfare and "troubles" have not fully achieved: the true unification of Turkish and Greek Cypriots. We think this is pure poppycock and that Dr. Vygotsky more likely has some criminal design in mind. Investigators understandably also took whatever else was of interest to them, leaving little behind except rubble. Dr. Vygotsky fled before his laboratory was sacked, is being sought for questioning, and is said to be armed and dangerous.*

"So Al, you are being on the lam!" laughed Melusina, after translating for the neurologist.

"Crap! They wrecked my lab. I'll need to start from scratch."

"Don't assume the worst," I said. "You may still get those Nobels."

This only deepened Albert's funk. "There's been a hitch but I don't want to talk about it."

We didn't ask. "Okay," I said, "let's get back in the Rover. We're off to Famagusta!"

Chapter Fourteen

THE ROAD TO FAMAGUSTA

"Does everybody here know about the siege of Famagusta?" asked Darcy, hogging the middle of the back seat while Gayle whizzed us down B16 through Ornithi, Vatali, Lysi, and Koúklia toward the fabled city.

"Yes, we all know," I said, "and don't wish to hear it all over again." Melusina was the world authority on Famagusta, having led a team of preservationists two years earlier in restoring a damaged museum there. She sighed.

Darcy launched his lecture. "Just in case anybody has forgotten some details, I'll rehearse the story. You, Albert, you know nothing about the siege of Famagusta. Science nerds know bollocks about history. Gayle, keep your eyes on the road! So this is the greatest single story in the history of the bloody Christians and the bloody Turks. It's gruesome as hell."

Albert stuffed pita in his ears.

"You see, Selim the Sot had a fondness for Commandaria and decided to invade Cyprus to enhance his wine cellar. He sent his mate Mustafa Pasha. A sneaky Muslim commander endowed with two hundred thousand warriors. Mustafa took the island in months, except Famagusta. Got that? On the way he slaughtered half the population of Nicosia and sent crates of heads back home. Selim rejoiced with every shipment. Could barrels of Commandaria be far behind? But the Venetian Christians under Marcantonio Bragadino put up a ten-month resistance, outnumbered four to one. The Turks fired thousands of cannonballs into the city. Bragadino sent out sorties to gather food when the supply of dogs, cats, and rats was running out—Must inject that starvation's no excuse for eating those poor critters—Mustafa invaded the Rivettina Bastion but the Venetians set off a landmine that buried one thousand Turks alive. Ha! So Mustafa was really pissed when Bragadino finally surrendered on August 1, 1571—yes, there will be a quiz—Despite guarantees of safe passage, Mustafa had his crack executioner cut off Bragadino's nose and ears, and ten days later had him flayed alive. Stuffed the skin with straw and paraded it through the streets. So began the glorious Ottoman reign of Cyprus, from 1571 to 1878. Then we Brits took pity and decided England's green and pleasant land should extend to the Karpaz peninsula. Forgot to say that Selim the Sot got drunk on the captured Commandaria and broke his neck in the bathtub. Ha!"

"Darcy, try to remember that you Brits get mixed reviews for your charities on behalf of Cyprus," I observed.

"We have a little time now before we get to Famagusta," said Darcy, ignoring my barb. "Would you like to hear *my* story?"

Silence.

"Brilliant. Here it is. I was born on July 20, 1974. Does that date mean anything to anybody?"

"It's the date of the Turkish invasion of Cyprus," I said. "Do you think it's symbolic or something?"

"No, it just means I'm younger than you. Also fitting that I'm the one to bail this island out."

"We're all here to bail it out," I said. "You've rescued the sea turtles, with an assist from Gaia, also assured the flourishing of mouflon, with an assist from testosterone. But Gayle has rescued the island from desertification, and Melusina has found the iconic Aphrodite, a source of pride for Cypriot Greeks and Turks alike.

Albert may have the answer to their ancient animosity. I'm putting Cyprus on the literary map again with Rimbaud's lost notebook. The profits will go to restoring Cypriot antiquities damaged by the Turks. Jasmine will continue her efforts to ban chips and get songbirds off taverna menus. So Darcy, you're not the only well-meaning genius in the Rover."

"I hear you, mate, but please no more interruptions." I maintained a diplomatic silence while Albert muttered a Yiddish obscenity under his breath. Darcy continued, "My father raised sheep while my mother made cheese at our farm in Shropshire. They wanted me to be an Anglican priest but I was a pagan from an early age. I liked that Jesus was a shepherd and carpenter but told my parents that turning water into wine was bollocks. Didn't know it then but my early childhood was like Gerald Durrell's. I was always collecting animals—bugs, snakes, worms, fireflies, turtles. I made friends with all the sheep and gave them names. No problem when they were sheared, but I cussed out my parents when my friends were sent off to the slaughterhouse, and I refused to eat the mutton my mother put on the table. Felt like cannibalism. My way of flirting was to hold up live bugs by their hind ends and stick them in girls' faces. I liked hearing them scream. Let's see—I was elected the most unpopular boy in primary school, then the most unpopular teenager in secondary school. Never had any dates. I liked my animals more than humans anyway and became England's youngest vegetarian. Had no Oxbridge ambitions and went to the Royal Veterinary College in London. Made my fame rescuing the Majorcan midwife toad from extinction. I bred the critters in captivity, released them all around Majorca, and encouraged the males to help out with the eggs. They were reluctant but signed on. Besides Gerald Durrell, my hero is Alexander von Humboldt, the world's greatest scientist nobody has ever heard of. To get some electric eels out of a South American swamp, he drove a herd of horses into the water to stir them up. Got nearly fatal shocks as he grabbed them for a better look. Yes, I like beasties more than people. Behold my success with Gayle up there. At least I've never stuck a bug in your face, luv. What does Bart have that I don't?"

Gayle ignored him.

"Not sure you've given us a deep insight into your character, Darcy—thing is, people rarely change," put in Jasmine. "You've always been pompous and obnoxious and always will be . . . Doesn't mean we can't keep up collaborating on the songbirds. They're more important than whether we like each other."

There was vitriol in this, because Jasmine had not forgotten Darcy's early rebuff of her in favor of the elusive Gayle. But I'm inclined to agree with her that people rarely change in fundamentals.

I suppose it was my turn but I wasn't about to tell them my story. As a writer I reveal myself only in my memoirs. This is one of them, so maybe I'll say something about me down the road.

Down the road? After the mudslide fiasco, we were delayed again a full week by one obstacle after another not worth the telling. When Famagusta came in sight we were ready to throttle one another, our august think tank reduced to a cage of skunks and weasels. When we stopped at a garage outside Famagusta, we picked up a new print-run of the *Pan-Cypriot Gazette* and found, to our relief, that Armide and Renaud had been found. She didn't require rescue because she was in love with her captor. Everything had accelerated. They were set to be married in Othello's Tower, called the citadel in the Shakespeare play, with pan-Cypriot press coverage and some three hundred honored guests, including the William Shakespeare impersonator. The mayor of Famagusta would officiate. An editorial celebrated the event as a historic merging of the Cypriot Greeks and Turks. Albert perked up. "Wake me when the call comes from Stockholm!"

Rancid and famished, we checked into Hotel Ouzini, ranked 193rd of the 193 hotels in the Famagusta district and best known for mosquitoes and inedible grub. Because of the influx of guests and press, there were no remaining rooms elsewhere. Six think-tank fellows in a single suite with one mosquito-ridden bathroom was a challenge, but we took turns in the shower and ordered in some meze, spoiled but ambrosial to the starving. Melusina was sensible enough not to push a polyamorous agenda. Even if we'd had a glamorous suite, Albert was a prudish killjoy, Gayle was uninterested, Darcy was a boor, Melusina was now unwilling to share Jasmine, and I was by nature a reserved observer.

We were cheered by the prospect of the wedding, scheduled in two weeks. The mayor had put out a call for donations so that Renaud and Armide might have proper wedding apparel and the city could furnish forth a wedding feast. I made a call to the Soros foundation and procured via PayPal the amount necessary, relaying it to the mayor, who thanked me by sending over a case of Commandaria and a sixteen-inch-high Doob of himself. We six ventured out to the Desdemona Bar and Grill, a windowless dive with a savory fifteen-platter meze, built into an old bastion. It was just down the street from the Lala Mustafa Pasa Camii, originally the Cathedral of St. Nicholas but renamed after the victorious flayer of Bragadino.

Getting wind of the imminent wedding, the Genealogy Roadshow had gone to work, interviewing Armide and Renaud, taking DNA samples from inside their cheeks, and on a hunch, comparing these with Bragadino's flayed skin, now in an urn in a Venetian church, also with DNA taken from inside Mustafa Pasha's turban, enshrined in a museum within the Rivettina Bastian, where the Venetians in 1571 waved the white flag of surrender. The Roadshow announced that Armide was a great-great-great-great-great-great-great-great-great-great-great-great-great-great-great granddaughter of Mustafa, while Renaud was a great-great-great-great-great-great-great-great-great-great-great-great-great-great-great grandson of Bragadino. Bragadino was, of course, Venetian and Roman Catholic or "Latin," not Greek Orthodox. But one of his granddaughters mated by mistake with a Greek Orthodox of surname Remis, thus explaining how Renaud, a Greek Orthodox, could be a direct descendant of the unfortunate Roman Catholic Venetian commander.

This would be a royal wedding of sorts, and a symbolic reconciliation of longtime adversaries. Darcy thought it comparable to how the York-Lancaster War of the Roses ended in the glorious House of Tudor.

Albert called a press conference where he took full credit for the union, explaining that romantic love had nothing to do with bringing the pair together. It was all owing to his serum. "These cretins cursed and stabbed one another until my serum kicked in. I expect worldwide distribution within two or three years and the cessation of all war."

"What will you do with the royalties, professor?"

"Invest them in my retirement fund, numbskull. You expect me to give anything away? I got no funding for Empathomax. It was the result of some pretty shrewd insights, *all my own*."

Albert seemed a bit nervous as he called the conference to a close, with no applause from the press for this redeemer not only of Cyprus but possibly of humankind. The *New York Times* carried the news, editorializing with an unprecedented cussword that an anti-aggression serum would be a milestone after two hundred thousand years of genocidal tribalism. "Let enhanced mirror-neuron synapses rescue the damned human race if nothing else can. Enough is enough!"

The next day we set out to explore the ghost town of Varósha to the south of Famagusta. In recent visits to the island, Melusina had led the Greek Cypriot negotiations with the Turkish occupiers for resettlement of the island's biggest eyesore. Varósha had sprung up after the Ottoman's triumph of 1571, eventually populated by some forty thousand Greek Cypriots no longer permitted within the old Venetian walls. In August 1974 they all deserted the town like scared flamingoes as they came under bombardment by the Turkish army, not even washing dishes or taking down laundry. They also left a number of shabby beach hotels that became even shabbier after the occupation. The Turks did little other than loot the city, not interested in fixing up hotels when they had plenty of empty beds in the north. Tourists at the southern hilltop of Dherínia could pay to view through binoculars the crumbling mess, infested with vermin and flourishing weeds. These were decaying structures, not picturesque ruins, but worth a euro to gape at.

When Melusina gained permission to enter the ghost town two years earlier, she led the team first to the archeological museum and was appalled, if hardly surprised, to find its antiquities looted and sold long ago on the black market. She began an international campaign for their interception and return. And she was a member of the pan-Cypriot team of negotiators who began the process of Greek Cypriot resettlement of the ghost town. We observed hundreds of people pounding away at their fixer-uppers. *This Old House* had featured many Varóshan structures that one might have thought beyond repair. With ample Sheetrock and human persistence, they became almost as livable as post–World War II Quonset huts.

Though Melusina was a world authority on the history and culture of Varósha, Darcy treated us to one of his history lectures, ending with, "This dump should be sucked up by a giant tornado and carried out to sea."

"Not so loud, Darcy," I cautioned. "Some of these people know English. They're doing their best to repair what history has given them."

"History. Who called it a 'bucket of ashes'?" asked Darcy.

"Samuel Butler," replied Gayle, most recent undergrad among us, if never an English major. "Carl Sandburg often gets the credit."

We entered the archeology museum, where a solitary clerk sitting under a naked light bulb welcomed us, recognizing the famed Melusina. "Miss Frei, everything in this museum is owing to you."

In the museum was not very much—a Mycenaean bowl, a faience rhyton from Kition, the skeleton of an ass buried alive at

Salamis, a bronze head of Zeus with silver eyeballs from Soléa, an ivory handle of a mirror showing a man attacking a lion from Koúklia. But Melusina had persuaded the Metropolitan Museum to return the great Cesnola collection. It would soon be installed here. She also initiated the rite of burning an effigy of Cesnola on his birthday. This made her a favorite of locals, both Greeks and Turks.

I hoped the roof would be repaired by then, the larger of the venomous snakes sent packing, and enough air-conditioning to prevent the fragile antique statuary from crumbling in the heat.

As we surveyed the few ancient objects now returned, we fell into a discussion of time. "Picasso hated time," I said. "Every brush stroke was defiance. These damaged antiquities show that nothing is exempt from time's rude wasting. Maybe I'm quoting Keats, eh, Gayle?"

She nodded. "I'm the youngest among us but live every day for the moment. My morning cocktail always makes me think of mortality. If I tempt fate by flying upside down, it's, well, the what-me-worry of the last days of Pompeii."

"Many thanks for treating us to the same sensation," snarled Darcy. "Me, I live for my animals. If I cark it I'm letting them down. Gerald Durrell's immortality is in his zoo, not those cutesy tales he cooked up to finance it."

Put in mind of the impersonators, I said, "It's sobering to think that all four greats are dead—Rimbaud at thirty-seven, Shakespeare at fifty-two, Gerald Durrell at seventy, Lawrence at seventy-eight. Nobody is exempt if they aren't. I don't find this consoling."

"I am having the longest view of time here," said Melusina. "For forty-six I am being pretty well preserved, right, Jasmine? But I am thinking in terms of millennia. Look at my Aphrodite—the world's best-preserved major antiquity. Along has come a geologist who is reminding me that the Pentelic marble carved by Pygmalion has predated him by four hundred million years. He has plunked down a twenty-four-foot tape measure and pointed to the final centimeter.

This was when Pygmalion began removing the excess marble, and the tape's very end was when I have unearthed her."

"Even your Aphrodite will disappear when protons decay a billion decillion years from now," muttered Albert. "Maybe sooner if the next generation doesn't give a hoot about art. Video games are everything now. The cessation of war will just give us more time for video games, video war games. Hmmm, I should invest."

"Jasmine," I remarked, "you haven't said much. What's your take on time?"

"A psychologist once told me I'm 'sensate discontinuous.' She adapted that from Jung. Most anorexics are sensate discontinuous because eating is sensate, so they prefer to discontinue it!" We laughed. "Not sure it made much sense."

We were approaching a small exhibition of Cypriot plank sculpture. Melusina exclaimed, "Jasmine, they are looking just like you, right down to skin color—and so skinny!"

Jasmine gave Melusina a quick pinch and continued, "As a nutritionist this is my view of time. It has to do with memory. You remember Proust and his madeleine dipped in tea? Memory isn't a coherent series of events like a story. If we're lucky it's a reservoir of luminous moments made up of sensations, images, moments that last for one reason or another—our *real* memories. They pop up in no order. My best ones are of chocolate cake."

"Wordsworth called them 'spots of time,'" I put in as group guru.

Jasmine nodded. "They station us in a flow of time that is otherwise meaningless, just one thing after another."

"I haven't known you were so philosophical a girlfriend," remarked Melusina. "How are you coming by this?"

"Took a philosophy course as an undergrad and I can still press the button. We Blacks are aware of color early on because others are always noticing ours, defining us in terms of it. That's sensate but mostly it's negative, pinning us to the wall."

"You Blacks have a color hierarchy—lighter skins are prized. Sounds racist to me," snorted Albert. "*Tsu zeyn zikher*, we Jews have hierarchies. Smaller noses are prized, otherwise why so many rhinoplasties?"

"It's all very sad," said Melusina. "But Jasmine, your turn, what's your story? I should know by now."

Lovers are well advised not to tell too much. Jasmine told just enough as we sweated together in the museum.

"I'm not HIV positive and no suicides in my family—so far. I was on the Genealogy Roadshow hoping to find my African roots not long after getting the genius award. Yes, I'm a genius—IQ one hundred and sixty-two—not bad for a Black nutritionist. The Nobelist William Shockley said we Blacks have average IQs of eighty-five, dull normals. He invented the transistor. Had an IQ of a hundred and twenty-eight—not enough to get into Mensa—and a moral IQ of zero. Racist pig!"

"You're going off story," interjected Melusina. "You're smart. You correct my German. But I'd like to know more about the person who has skinny limbs haunting me the night through."

"Cool it, girl." Jasmine turned back to the group. "The genealogists confirmed I'm Cameroonian, with ancestors sold into slavery by loving neighboring tribes to the Portuguese. They were forced to strip, get rubbed over with slime, and sold to the highest bidders. One horse could get you ten shackled slaves. Best thing about me is I'm the twelfth great-granddaughter on my mother's side of John Punch."

"John Punch?" asked Melusina.

"The first official slave in the English colonies, Virginia 1640. He was smart, really smart. Guess who's his eleventh great-grandson."

"I'll go with Jay-Z," said Gayle.

"Close, but not that famous. It's Barack Obama, remember him? We're cousins. Maybe this explains my IQ."

"Never am I imagining I have been sleeping with a cousin of Barack Obama!" said Melusina. "This is making it better."

"I'm not so sure," put in Darcy. "High IQs put me in mind of that bastard Hitler and eugenics."

"Let's not be talking about Hitler," sighed Melusina.

"You must know," I said, "that the United States beat Hitler to the punch with the nineteenth-century Oneida Community, right there in prim upstate New York. We should all visit sometime."

"Quit interrupting, dude," Jasmine said. "Back to my story. I grew up the only child in a middle-class Black family that tried its best to assimilate. My father was a Roto-Rooter vice president. Voted for Goldwater and the W! Thank God he drew a line at— can't say his name. My mother was a social worker and secretly voted Democratic. Must have been the John Punch in her. She and my father were distant, but Mom and I were close. She had a drinking problem and one day she was drunk enough to tell me a secret—she was having quickies at the office. This made me feel sort of sorry for my father but I could understand it. He was cold and withholding. I'd try anything to get his attention back then. Pathetic. That's when I became anorexic and almost died, trying to get my parents to eat cake while I ate none. Go figure."

"You're still trying to get others to eat!" said Darcy. "Or telling them what the blinking hell not to eat. But go on with you."

"Talk therapy didn't cure my anorexia, so my parents fired the Jungian. What worked was CBT—"

"Right you are!" cried Darcy. "I use cognitive behavioral therapy on raccoons and bats with attention deficit disorder."

"At the hospital they made me stand naked in front of a mirror ten minutes every day. Problem was, I had this delusion that the skinnier I got, the more beautiful. I was a mess. No tits or ass, and for a Black I was pale. No energy, no periods, no nothing. But I got the picture. So I began to eat again, especially the chocolate cake my mom smuggled in, and I put on enough to get out. I became a nutritionist, just like crazy people become psychotherapists. My stint in Indiana seeing what obese bumpkins ate made me a zealot. Meanwhile, my father discovered my mother's extracurriculars and divorced her. She came home one day reeking of Old Spice and he got the truth out of her. That was tough on me, made me wary of marriage. See, Melusina, I was vulnerable to your advances because you weren't proposing *marriage*."

"You're still skinny as a broom," put in Gayle. "Are you fully cured?"

"Anorexics are always borderline, girl. But that's why Melusina and I are a good match. I'm lean and she's cream. But we got off the subject of time. I'm thirty-two and want to store up more luminous moments, like swimming with Melusina when we uncovered the Aphrodite and attending the Royal Wedding. The air is promise-crammed—the Shakespeare impersonator said that to me, one of the lines he got right. I plan to edit out all the bad stuff from my memory bank. Cheerful people have a knack for this. Depressives wake up at four in the morning and rehearse everything that's gone wrong. Not for me."

Intermezzo. I must be a depressive because this is exactly what I do. At 4:00 a.m. I weigh the calamities for which I wasn't responsible against those for which I was. More sinned against than sinning? Probably not. My sin was one of omission—I never felt passionate love, at best just strong affection. But love or affection, isn't it true that most romantic relationships that don't last end badly? As I go down my list of old girlfriends and wives, I check off the few good moments—like out-performing other males at charades, trying to get lost together in the woods, managing to keep a hard-on—and edit out the endings, recriminations, and cold turkeys. What I don't understand is how somebody like Lawrence Durrell could have all that casual sex and emerge with himself and others unscathed, leaving only his two wives and one daughter permanently damaged or dead. I don't presume you readers take an interest in me beyond my ability to tell a tale, and this memoir is no confessional. But maybe now is the time to say a few words.

For starters, I've been married and divorced three times with one kid by each spouse—and none of these six people is in touch with me. I'll explain as best I can.

I was bored out of my mind until I was ten and we packed off for Cyprus.

Four years on the island were a revelation. Public school began early in the morning and consisted mostly of breaks, until we were released shortly after one in the afternoon and ran like bulldogs through the streets... My playmates were eager to teach me the language, and I quickly picked up Greek for *snot, fart, kick, hard-on, fist, gun,* and *boobs.* But it was the weekend outings with my parents to beaches and small villages that fastened Cyprus forever in my memory as an enchanted isle.

When the Turks invaded, I learned that ethnic differences are not simply exotic and charming but the source of hatred and blood-letting. I could hear the bombs and machine guns, and see the smoke, destroyed buildings, and occasional corpse on the street. This was a true loss of innocence that changed me on every level.

When we returned to Ottawa, I became a teenage punk. This may have contributed to my father's early demise. I collected Sex Pistol singles, learned from them how to spit in airports. I played hooky and lost my virginity in a choir pew to a girl planning to enter a nunnery the following week. I like to think that she was having a final splurge before the portal shut forever and that I was more seduced than seducing. But who knows?

I got into MIT on scholarship and moved into a one-bedroom apartment. This was before the internet, so I had to think of other ways of being bad. But in Cambridge in the late seventies it was impossible not to be bad, even for a Canadian. This was the decade of bad taste in clothes and furnishings, as in morals. I wore gaudy designer jackets with broad lapels and yellow polyester shirts, and graced my living room with a shag rug. Because I had a car and stopped spitting, girls took to me. I'd have as many as three girlfriends at a time and became a master at double and triple dealings, not without some regret, also shame at the thought of getting caught.

I read Rimbaud, who in his private life was so bad he made the Sex Pistols sound like a church choir. I stayed on at MIT and got my doctorate in sociolinguistics, writing a dissertation, "Fourth Language Acquisition among Canadian Inuit."

I had settled down my senior year, shortening my list of girlfriends. After graduating I began a string of bad marriages. I'll be brief. I married only native-speaking foreigners, in part to learn their languages and customs. But as I've confessed, it's always the exotic that pulls on me, as someone for whom Ottawa didn't answer to experiential yearnings. You might say I'm attracted only by those who don't remind me of me.

My first marriage was to an Italian, Annunziata Abbandonato, from Naples on a two-year Fulbright to study engineering at MIT. Science didn't dispel dogma. A committed Catholic, she refused sex before marriage and was disappointed on our wedding night in Salem. I blamed it on my faulty ordnance but she, of a superstitious nature, thought she'd been bewitched and blamed me for a honeymoon in a town famed for witches. This didn't prevent her from getting pregnant right away. An atheistic ex-Catholic and a devout Catholic do not a good match make, even if they become parents. I am not at all a morning person, and her early rising for Mass meant I began every day with a pillow over my head, a drooling infant, and Ann's warm prophecy, before slamming the door, that I'd never find my way out of the Inferno. One day I returned from class to find she'd absconded with our infant daughter, Bernadetta, and left no note.

I learned from the engineering department that she was en route back to Naples, apparently resolved that a Canadian husband and a degree in engineering were not her path. I never heard from her again and was left with a mildly broken heart, for she had large brown eyes that always seemed to express astonishment, an endearing inability to order anything other than cheese ravioli whenever we dined out, and a personality so inscrutable that I could project onto her anything I liked. Who she was in essence I have no idea. But I rallied by writing a memoir of Naples, which I had never visited. *Neapolitan Fright Nights*—so titled by my prescient editor—was my entry into the publishing world. Midlisted, it assured a career of modest advances from one publisher or another.

You'd think this early marital disaster would have immunized me against more marriages, but no. My second wife, Nadezhda Novoseltseva, was my entrée to Moscow in 1980, nine years before the collapse of the Soviet Union. A niece of Mikhail Gorbachev, then a member of the Politburo and five years short of his ascension to the presidency, she'd been admitted to Radcliffe where she majored in political science, what else? I'd finished my doctorate and was asked to serve as mentor at a Radcliffe dormitory. She was a senior when I met her, and Radcliffe seniors in those days panicked if they hadn't found a mate from within the paddock of Harvard or MIT by the time they were pushed out onto the real world racetrack. Wouldn't anybody they met thereafter be a comedown from the elite bloodlines of the Cambridge community? This silly fear infected Nad, contemptuous of young Russian males whom she regarded as louts and slobs, even though she judged the great Russian writers and composers as superior to everybody the West had to offer, whether Shakespeare, Bach, Goethe, Beethoven, or Austen. Wishing to learn Russian and quite taken by her histrionic Slavic melancholy, precocious in someone so young, I proposed the day before graduation.

I proved a misfit in Moscow, where I was taken for an evangelical Christian missionary who had hoodwinked one of their own. I tried to convince the KGB as well as our neighbors that there were few Anabaptists in Canada, and that I was every bit as atheistic as Karl Marx. I had talked myself into atheism at the age of eight when our priest couldn't answer a simple question, Why does God have a beard? But most were somehow convinced that, after two years of sitting on my hands, supposedly teaching English as a second language, I'd begin targeting Russian Orthodox devotees, soft targets because already emotional theists. Nad's fun and engaging uncle was too busy rising in the Politburo and fending off gangsters to lend a hand, let alone socialize with us, and Nad began to tire of defending me. My visa was mysteriously canceled and I could either leave the country or do jail time, maybe forever. Nad decided to stay in Moscow, keeping our baby boy, Bogdan, conceived during our cheerless honeymoon on the Black Sea. She claimed she would miss me, and I made do with this limited expression of loss. I rallied by converting my Muscovite notebook into another memoir, titled by my sagacious editor *Beluga Blues*.

Finally there was Charusmita Chakraborty, a Hindu from Calcutta, or Kolkata if you'd rather, whom I met at an AA meeting when I was teaching creative nonfiction at the Iowa Writer's Workshop in Iowa City. Like most midlist authors I had turned to drink and was obsessed with keeping my modestly selling titles in print when I should just have kept on writing. Unusual in a Hindu, Char had turned to drink because life in Iowa City was so dull after the routine frenzy of street life in Calcutta. She was working toward a master's in Business Administration and making ends meet as waitperson in an Indian restaurant on South Dubuque. There, she began taking surreptitious sips of Bombay gin to cope with the affective flatness and twang of her Midwestern customers, whose vacuous talk she couldn't help but overhear. Her own English was superior, so we felt an immediate bond in knowing we were a cut above these hicks.

Maybe this was an insufficient romantic connection but we decided to marry. I expressed a wish to get the hell out of Iowa and return with her to Calcutta, where I would teach English as a second language and continue a self-delusion that I had something in common with James Joyce. Clients were difficult to find because everybody in India already spoke English. Right away she conceived a girl, Bhagyalakshmi, and all seemed to be going well enough as I absorbed Hindi and the culture of Calcutta, while she ran an Uber outfit from home.

I respected Char's practice of ahimsa, the avoidance of cruelty to living creatures, including slaughtering and eating cows. But I slipped and was spotted by one of her brothers eating a Quarter Pounder with Cheese at a newly opened McDonald's on State Street. Upon hearing this, Char ceased having sex, saying that my flesh was polluted by the suffering of the many cows murdered for my hamburger, and it would be one year before we could resume marital rites. I readily consented.

Another revealing blunder was a culturally anachronistic assumption I made at the funeral pyre of her father, a vegetarian who'd suffered a sudden heart attack. I falsely believed Char's mother was about to leap onto the pyre in keeping with the long-banned practice of sati, the suicide of Hindu wives at the funeral of their husbands. In fact she had only stumbled over a small marsh mongoose that strayed up to the pyre, maybe hoping for baked funeral meats, when I grabbed her from certain death. Char thanked me but felt I saved her mother only because of a colonialist stereotype.

I made other blunders I won't bother to narrate. Usually I'm better at cultural assimilation. Char got a divorce on grounds of marital neglect, winning possession of our daughter.

Another reason? The fact is, I failed to love my wives fully, and they sensed it. There's no such thing as a duty to *love*—ask Kant and Coleridge—but I'd signed on to marriage, so I was in moral peril for merely *liking*.

Returning to Cambridge I continued in the same manner, always suffering *Sehnsucht* and keeping a suitcase next to my front door in case opportunity arose for travel abroad. My memoir of Calcutta, *Holy Cow!!!*, so titled by my esteemed editor, was midlisted but garnered some favorable reviews, mostly in *Briefly Noted*.

You may have registered that all three marriages were sabotaged also by religious fundamentalism.

I've not dwelt on my own mother, who was hardly my enemy but became for me the symbolic equivalent of Ottawa. I kept up a perfunctory correspondence with her over the years, editing out all the more engaging—because incriminating—moments of my life. I don't know more about coincidence beyond the fact that life seems largely governed by it. My mother died of a stroke the very moment, I would learn, that overseas I rescued Charusmita's mother from the funeral pyre. Physicists might call this "spooky action at a distance" or in this case, to coin a phrase, "reverse entanglement"—the demise of one photon reignites the life of its partner. I felt more guilt than grief and wished I could somehow have rescued her also. I was then a total orphan without the illusion that parents protect one from the great leveler because they must go first.

As for getting out of marriages, or more precisely being dumped from them, I decided to stop seeking a spouse for new habitats and languages. Frankly it had begun to feel exploitative. My two subsequent midlisted cultural memoirs were written after solitary journeys to countries cordial to Canadians.

As I read over this thumbnail sketch I feel it oversimplifies a fairly complex sensibility, so I'm getting a bit defensive. I'm widely read in many languages. I've studied the great philosophers and have the welfare of the human race in mind, seen in my think tank itself. I'm deeply curious and believe I'm capable of warm connections if not fiery.

Lord Byron asks what is left of basic human life after one subtracts all the daily buttoning and unbuttoning, and his brilliant reply is "the summer of a dormouse." I've packed in more than a dormouse but as I've become older, approaching seventy as I write, I feel my rather busy life has too often meant getting out of things— out of town, out of marriages, out of foreign ports of call, out of the many physical maladies I've not even mentioned because so humdrum. Freud would say that my droll humor is a tactic for protecting a fragile ego from potential threats. Maybe he would say the same of Lord Byron, self-exiled from England in 1816 only to return pickled in a wooden barrel in 1824. His humor was nothing if not droll.

Writing is itself protective against the greatest threat—leaving black-on-white traces of oneself in the face of ineluctable time and death. It's a grand illusion—*ars longa, vita brevis*—the sweetest cheat.

But I'd add something defiant. The story I'm telling is a parable of human life in the demented early twenty-first century, not a *jeu d'esprit*, if packaged like one. When you've turned the last page or fingered your way to the last frame on your accursed Kindle, think over what you've read and maybe you'll agree.

I'll step aside now and get on with my story for I sense in my readership an impatience with literary metaphysics.

— *Chapter Fifteen* —

ALBERT'S DILEMMA

Albert announced that all this talk about time bored him and he was getting hungry, so we headed back to the Desdemona where we took most of our meals in the lead-up to the Royal Wedding. It was a busy time for us all. Albert interviewed the royal couple and administered a booster serum just to insure the match would hold. Melusina helped Armide with her Islamic wedding apparel. Though a meteorologist, Gayle took a collateral interest in seismic activity, some of which had been recently reported in the Famagusta area. She obtained some rudimentary equipment through Amazon Prime to make measurements of her own. We spent lots of time touring the city and made an obligatory daytrip north to Salamis. Albert declined to go along, reminding us that Jews were banished from Cyprus in AD 116 and weren't readmitted until the late nineteenth century, the most sustained run of programmatic anti-Semitism ever.

"So, Al, you are having an interest in history after all!" quipped Melusina.

"The story goes that Jews massacred the entire Gentile population of Salamis in 116. There may be some lingering bad feeling. I'm not going."

"Weird to think of Jews slaughtering instead of being slaughtered," put in Darcy.

"*Oy gevalt*, we must have had our reasons," replied Albert. "Anyway, I've got another press conference."

A word about *why* another press conference. We all sensed that Albert had been preoccupied by something or other from the beginning of his stay in Cyprus. He was always checking his cell and this was no teenage addict. He'd receive calls at odd hours and creep into the washroom so no one could hear him, except for the occasional Yiddish cusswords: "*Kacken zee ahf deh levanah!*" "*Tuches arine!*" "*Kozebupkes!*"—too gross to translate. Something was going on, for he seemed unhinged.

The *New York Times* broke the news on page one just three days before the wedding. Albert was accused of both plagiarism and fudging his experimental results. These accusations were brought by a pair of Estonian neurologists—Koit Kraanvelt and Sula Soosaar—recently denied tenure at the University of Kentucky. The esteemed journal *Science* was considering repudiation of the peer-reviewed article in which Albert set forth the biochemical preliminaries that underlay his experiment with human subjects and Empathomax.

You might well ask how one could be accused of plagiarism if experimental results were fudged. Isn't this like trying to gain possession of a piece of rotten fruit? This was the defense Albert mounted.

The next day the fired profs explained matters. Albert had used logarithmic shortcuts in making the case that mirror neurons could be enhanced, making use of their own data in this field. One of the accusers had a nine-year-old son addicted to computer games—he spotted the statistical distortion Albert had smoothed over.

It's not easy to arrest an errant scientist, but the president of Rockefeller University said she was looking into the matter and convening a committee to determine if scientific fraud had been committed and whether Albert should be demoted to clinical assistant professor.

Freshly back from a visit to the royal tombs of Salamis, where servants and horses were sacrificed whenever a royal kicked off, and, to judge by their grimaces and hand-and-foot binding, not having gone gentle into that good night—for does this make any sense?—I asked Albert, "Is there any truth in these charges? The Soros foundation has asked me to put you on probation."

"No truth, none. The counter-evidence is Armide and Renaud. Those Estonian schnooks just don't want me to get the call from Stockholm. Scientists are only less than human. Political crap is as common in the NSF as the House of Representatives. Take it from me, Mister Beasley, I'm for real."

"Okay, Albert, I'll believe you until you are thoroughly disgraced."

The thought occurred to me that such a disgrace would make for a more engaging memoir of the Cyprus Think Tank. Maybe this narrative could use more chicanery. I left this thought unexpressed, patted Albert on the shoulder, and told him to relax and look forward to the Royal Wedding.

"Renaud has asked me to be best man," said Albert, "and that's what I am—best man!"

Chapter Sixteen

THE ROYAL WEDDING

Othello's Tower, where the couple would marry, was part of the massive Venetian fortification that resisted the Turkish siege of 1571. Armide and Renaud, direct descendants of the principals, were in effect nullifying the infamous siege in a ritual of reunification. The tower had a great hall, recently cleared of some of its rats and pigeons, with a large stage where the procession through the courtyard would end and the ceremony would take place.

Part of the mystique of the tower lay in the treasure the Venetian merchants stored there when it became clear the Turks would prevail. The Turks searched for it day and night over the centuries. Countless dowsers, diviners, and whirling dervishes were deployed, as well as rubble-clearing slaves, but the gold was never found.

The think-tank fellows put on rental Sunday penitentials and walked to the tower for the ceremony the afternoon of August 18, 2024, passing under the renowned Lion of St. Mark at the portal. I went along in drag, wearing a brown *kouroukla*, or female headdress, and a damask *saiya*, a Cypriot frock that Melusina requested be tailored for ease of breastfeeding. I took this precaution out of fear that Renaud would remember me as the rake who splashed Armide on *Kataklysmós*, and her flirtatious retaliation. *Better safe than dead*, I figured.

The tower was crowded on Sunday with honored guests and press corps. I recognized many from the unveiling of the Aphrodite. Helium balloons gave buoyancy to the long windowless chamber with encrusted limestone rib vaulting. Albert went forward to greet Renaud while the rest of us stayed in the rear to be inconspicuous. Renaud had undergone quite a makeover. He was dressed in a purple silk shirt, finely pressed black *vraka*—broad cotton trousers—and a velvet *zimbouni*—a fancy waistcoat. He wore an embroidered belt with a knitted purse attached that, by tradition, concealed a dagger. He embraced Albert, kissing each cheek, as the two followed the mayor down the middle of the courtyard, trailed by Renaud's Greek Cypriot proud, bewildered parents, siblings, and extended family. The Shakespeare impersonator was making a cameo appearance and joined the party on stage, looking much like Prospero.

Sorry I cannot tell you more about Renaud Remis's backstory. Not wishing to be taken for an informant, I never tried to find out. He will remain a blank unless you dare look him up.

It must have been a hand-me-down from the British occupation, but the ragtag local band cobbled together for the occasion played Elgar's "Pomp and Circumstance" with a cacophony that echoed throughout the tower and agitated the remaining rats and pigeons.

Then entered the bride, followed by her proud, bewildered parents, siblings, and extended family. Armide was swathed in an elaborate niqab. One would have thought this outfit befitting a traditional Muslim bride except that this niqab was a brilliant crimson velvet. Cypriot brides traditionally wear a red scarf to distinguish themselves from the nonbrides and to denote virginity, but Armide had gone apocalyptic with red. Attendees gasped at her audacity.

Joined at the altar, Armide and Renaud stood before the mayor, who fortunately spoke both Greek and Turkish. The bride and groom were slow learners, and their courtship had been nonverbal. Well, there's little that body language, plus some gasps, cannot communicate. Albert's own body language, with his head turned to the ceiling, implied that he was sole proprietor of the spectacle.

The mayor was asked to give an ecumenical twist to the readings, some taken from the Qur'an, others from the Eastern Orthodox Bible. Then he got down to business and managed to ignore the dragonfly that buzzed over his shoulder as if reading along.

In Turkish: "Do you, Armide the Muslim, accept Renaud the Christian as your lawfully wedded, uh, spouse?" He was politically correct and used the neutral Turkish *tureng* for "spouse" instead of *husband*.

"Sure thing! Like, he's cool!" she replied.

In Greek: "Do you, Renaud, take as your virgin bride the fair Armide?"

"Yes," he replied. "She's the bee's pajamas." *Pajama* is of Arabic origin, so there was a faint promise of verbal crossover.

"And because this ceremony is ecumenical and without a canonical script," said the mayor slyly—in Greek, then in Turkish— "where do you dears intend to spend your honeymoon?"

"We'll be staying in La Cavocle near the rocks of Aphrodite," replied Armide with warmth. "Every morning I'll swim three times around the rocks to restore my virginity. Over two weeks I'll lose my virginity fourteen times, a world record."

Hearing this, the Turkish Cypriots among the audience applauded. The entire ceremony was being videoed and within hours had gone viral, with millions of viewers pressing the "like" icon, some the "love." So began a fad of ethnic intermarriages the world over, arguably more important than legalistic resettlement issues on this particular island. It also resulted in flocks of women of all ages journeying from distant lands to the Aphrodite rocks to regain their virginity, whether in part or whole.

The recessional completed, we all entered into feasting and dancing within the tower, the ghosts of Othello and Desdemona having been dispersed into the grim rib vaulting. The families of bride and groom danced together so merrily that one would never have guessed there had been ethnic bickering on this island. I was asked by four middle-aged Greek and Turkish males to dance the *sirtaki* and the *halay*, which I pulled off as best as I could manage as a sixty-four-year-old Canadian male in drag. The Shakespeare impersonator danced alone, performing a totally inappropriate Elizabethan galliard and singing "'Tis Hymen peoples every town." Nobody approached him for fear of sucking up to the world's greatest literary celebrity. Gayle watched me with amusement as I improvised and shook my hips, strutting like a native with my skirts swirling and swaying.

But her expression changed when we all felt some shaking that was not the consequence of stomping around in native footwear. She was the first to know what was happening.

"Earthquake!" she cried. Then shouts of "Earthquake!" in English, Greek and Turkish, then a stampede for the portal, during which, somehow, nobody got trampled. Albert, who'd been a proud wallflower during the dancing, was the first to evacuate. "No death before Stockholm!" he cried as I witnessed him waddle off with remarkable speed for someone with a Groucho Marx slouch.

Gayle and I were side by side. "We were due for an earthquake," she explained matter-of-factly. "Last major one was in 15 BCE, and we're on a plate fracture five miles deep. I'd rate this only a 6.7, probably not very extensive." We managed to pass through the portal and looked back at the crumbling tower, where the Lion of St. Mark was now upside down.

"But look!" I said, wobbling with the aftershocks, "it was strong enough to cave in the west rampart."

We beheld the large collapsed structure with all the other escapees, who were mumbling about the earthquake being some kind of chastisement for intermarriage. The question was, which god did it? The Christian or the Muslim?

Though there was some residual gentle rain from Gayle's powder and no sun, we shielded our eyes because there, in all radiance, was a pile of Venetian gold—ingots, jewelry, coins, a life-sized statue of Caterina Cornaro fashioned of pure gold, and a golden swirly cat twenty times normal size, for the first domestic cats were bred in Cyprus. The quake had opened an ancient ventilation shaft, overlooked by the Turks, where the Venetian merchants had cleverly stashed their treasure.

The mayor had an over-the-top mike and laid claim to the fortune with Greek and Turkish equivalents of "finders keepers, losers weepers." But since the ceremony as well as the quake itself was being live-fed to worldwide social media, it didn't take more than a few minutes for a delegation of the pan-Cypriot government to come upon the scene in squeaky tanks that we Canadians had left behind after the 1974 invasion. They roped off the treasure, claiming it for the island as a whole.

Instead of declaring the vindictiveness of one god or another, everyone began saying the quake was a miracle. Damage beyond the tower was minimal. It was as if the quake targeted the tower alone, and the timing could not have been better.

Seven dumpsters were called in by authorities to pick up the loot and haul it to the island treasury in Nicosia. Melusina presided over the more fragile artifacts, doing a quick inventory of gold bracelets, earrings, daggers, and dildos.

While this was taking place, Armide and Renaud hopped aboard their moped and sped off to La Cavocle, so Armide would waste no time losing and regaining her virginity.

When the dumpsters had been loaded up and weighed, the gold tipped the scale at eighteen metric tons, hardly the equal of Fort Knox but enough for Cyprus to pay off its entire national debt and, as a gesture of goodwill, the entire Greek debt as well. All taxes were suspended, there was a well-financed operation to clear up the debris left by the 1974 invasion, there was reforestation of all patches in the Tróödos laid bare by the copper industry over the centuries, the shoddy tourist hotels were leveled and replaced with earthquake-resistant structures, all museums got adequate signage, and the Brits were paid off to shut down their two fatuous military bases.

I'm skipping ahead since these reforms took many months. And yes, I'm well aware that the earthquake and aftermath smack of *deus ex machina*. If nothing else works, call in an earthquake that uncovers Venetian gold. But remember this is a world of contingency where coincidence is King. So conceived, the earthquake was in keeping with strict literary realism, as was that tsunami occasioned by an earthquake a few chapters back. Shakespeare understood this well enough—only the unreflecting would say, "The plot was contrived, too coincidental . . . Desdemona carelessly loses the handkerchief that means so much to Othello, and Emilia innocently gives it to Iago who now has the prop he needs . . . Gimme a break!"—but the chance event, unpredictable because of the infinite manifold of possibilities, becomes Fate itself the moment it has happened. In this sense, finding the Venetian gold at just the right moment was destiny.

The think-tank fellows felt pretty good about the whole thing. We'd already done lots in rescuing the island, and surely we deserved some credit. But there were a couple of problems still to address, in case you've forgotten them—the Cypriot diet and those poor tasty songbirds, to which I now turn.

— *Chapter Seventeen* —

THE WINE FESTIVAL

AT LIMASSOL

It was time to head the Rover to the Limassol Wine Festival, an annual event celebrating Dionysus, the god of wine, for ten days, beginning in late August, during which the prostitution trade takes in a sum equivalent to the rest of the year, like Black Friday in the States. The festival keeps lackluster Limassol on the map, for it is otherwise known only for the flatulent container ships floating listlessly in its harbor and the topless bars catering to seedy Russian businessmen. The most colorful moment in its history occurred in 1191 when Richard the Lionheart subjugated the entire island, decapitating only as many locals as was seemly for a Christian.

It's time to back up a bit. Jasmine was at first into Darcy—brash, British, and vegetarian. But Darcy was himself smitten with adventurous, politically-minded Gayle, who took a liking to me, for there is no accounting for tastes. Jasmine and Darcy agreed, however, to collude on the matter of the Cypriot diet and the massacre of innocent songbirds.

Darcy had new notches in his belt, for the Minister of the Interior announced that all female mouflon on the island were pregnant and the sea turtle hatchlings had made it to the sea in record numbers. Some members of the pan-Cypriot legislature expressed concern that mouflon might blossom to become in Cyprus what kangaroos are in Australia, a weed animal.

As a nutritionist Jasmine had close ties with food engineers at the Culinary Institute of America. A few weeks before the wine festival, with Darcy's encouragement, she had shipped them a single pickled songbird named Procne and asked them to fabricate a vegetarian equivalent that could fool even an epicure like Lord Byron. It was great sport for Cypriots of all stripes to set traps of nylon mist or sticks filled with tree bark glue. Twelve million songbirds were trapped in 2002 alone, and that number had only increased over the years. We have the Knights Templar to thank for introducing this brand of avian genocide. Locals sell the birds to tavernas for pickling. A single pickled songbird can then be swallowed whole by a patron for three euros. Yum.

Food chemists went to work on Procne at the culinary institute and within a few weeks fabricated an identical faux songbird made entirely of Cypriot vegetables—black-eyed peas, courgettes, okra, cauliflower, radish, cabbage, garlic, eryngo, purslane, and a secret ingredient needed to bond these into a glop that settled in a birdlike mold. Attaching fake feathers and beaks then presented a challenge, also inserting unevacuated digestive tracks. But these were simply a matter of food engineering. The Soros foundation chartered an old turboprop to carry 120 million of the fakes to Limassol in time for the wine festival.

Darcy spoke for the think tank on a stage in the Anexartisías Mall at opening festivities and said the Soros foundation was donating 120 million songbirds in honor of all the progress the island had made with the sea turtles, the mouflon, the cultural reconciliation of North and South, desertification, the discovery of Pygmalion's Aphrodite, the national debt, and the Minister of the Interior's recent ban of chips. Darcy's jaunty voice dropped when he mentioned the ban.

By the way, Darcy had arranged for tourists to witness the arrival of the sea turtles via a virtual-reality submersion experience, all the better because it could be experienced any time of the year. This tactic warded off what would have been a revolt in the tourist industry, which so much depended on visitors thrilling to the sight of turtles laying eggs.

I've given you a summary, not a verbatim account, of Darcy's speech because it was pompous and irritating.

For the next ten days, thousands of Cypriots engorged themselves with songbirds, never noticing they were fakes—along with thousands of liters of the island's wines, the best of which I feel is the red Othello with its sturdy tannins and chocolate minerality. Among whites, Arsinoë is stellar with its midpalate, well-balanced short finish and hints of seaweed. The real drunks supplemented such wines with the more potent zivanía. There was dancing in the streets and fornication on the beach.

Not all was well as the festival drew on. We fellows heard a rumor spread over Greek and Turkish FM frequencies by pundits whose voices had an odd buzzing sonority. By sending enough pickled songbirds to last a decade, the Soros foundation would surely undermine the local songbird economy. If these morsels could now be had for free, how could they be sold to tavernas? And why not have both pickled songbirds *and* chips? Damn the Brits for mostly everything, but a majority of Cypriots felt their one great legacy was chips. And chips were now forbidden as a public-health menace on a par with Morton Cream Pie.

In response to these broadcasts as well as to posts on Facebook, Instagram, YouTube, and Twitter, the mood of the crowd slowly shifted against the think tank. There was talk of militias being formed, of our being tarred and feathered, or maybe flayed, hanged, and quartered in the best Turkish tradition.

"Come on, let's bail," whispered Gayle as we six crouched in an alleyway, watching the happy crowd metamorphose into a mob, Turks and Greeks now united against a common enemy—us. I called into Soros for a Comanche helicopter, which appeared as quickly as an Uber. Albert hung on to Darcy's right arm as we boarded amid the splatter of rotten produce that the jeering Cypriots were pitching our way. As we looked down while wiping off fruit and eggs, we witnessed Cypriot Greeks and Turks alike shaking fists at us as if we were politicians.

"Shouldn't you weigh our good deeds against our bad?" I shouted, "and fund a commemorative plaque in our honor, maybe to be placed on the High Line in Nicosia?"

Gayle put a hand over my mouth. "Bart, they can't hear you and they don't read lips. Keep your dumbass head down." This was timely advice because a zealot on the ground had accessed an old AK-47, it would seem, and splintered a good deal of glass around the cabin. Fortunately, he missed the fuel tank and we all survived, even if we were disgruntled at the way we'd been given the heave-ho by the very folk we had endeavored to save.

— *Chapter Eighteen* —

OUT OF CYPRUS

It is early fall of 2030, six years after the events disclosed so far. I will bring you up to date on the principals as well as the impersonators. As for Cyprus itself, I'll say little since you surely scan the daily digitals and already know what has happened with the island in the aftermath of our efforts to rescue it. But I'll quickly review some of it.

Soon after their wedding, Armide and Renaud were elected the duumvirate of the pan-Cypriot government. They wished to extend much of the think tank's program, without the taint of outsider intervention or even, as was claimed by many islanders, American hegemony. For a while, all went well. The duumvirate quickly produced four offspring. Once a month Armide flew from Nicosia to Páphos where she swam three times around the rocks of Aphrodite, flanked by aquatic bodyguards. The nearby Aphrodite of Pygmalion on Yeronisos became the island's principal tourist attraction. Every pagan on Earth was required to make a pilgrimage at least once in a lifetime.

Though much of my memoir with respect to romance was a case study in nonreciprocation, two marriages came to pass. Jasmine and Melusina secretly wedded in Manhattan within a week of our escape from the island. Gayle and I served as witnesses and off they flew to La Fonda hotel in Santa Fe for their honeymoon. Melusina swore off polyamory forever while Jasmine promised to eat more.

Over the next few years they merged their professional interests as well as bodies. Jasmine took up food archeology, specializing in coprolites of early Homo sapiens and Neanderthals. In 2027, she published *The Cave Woman's Diet*, which was the world's number-one best seller, flying off bookshelves in Cyprus and elsewhere and reducing, for a few months, the average waistline of women the world over.

For her part Melusina undertook African archeology and found evidence of ancient advanced civilizations, supporting disputed claims in *The Lost Cities of Africa* of ancient African advanced civilizations. With help from Gayle and yet another Soros-modified Cessna, she discovered a buried kingdom in Cameroon, some fifty miles east of Yaoundé, to which Jasmine traced her slave lineage. Carbon-fourteen dating disclosed that the city-state flourished simultaneously with Sumer and had a cuneiform language that linguists are now trying to decipher. Histories of the origins of writing are all rendered obsolete, to the despair of their scholars. The exact location is being kept secret to prevent looting. "I see wonderful, wonderful things!" Melusina exclaimed when she entered the first tomb. The exact nature of the artifacts has not yet been disclosed. A large carefully guarded repository has been erected for their temporary storage.

When we returned to the States after our humiliating expulsion from Cyprus and witnessed the marriage of Jasmine and Melusina, Gayle asked if she might stay a week or so at my Carmine Street apartment before returning to California, where she would teach a doctoral seminar on climate change. I was a bit wary but said yes, thinking that at least there was something to be said for having a houseguest because it compels one to rediscover one's own backyard. We confronted what remained of my apartment, subleased for the summer to two male NYU law students who had their eyes set on medical malpractice litigation. The only worse vandals are PKs—you know, preacher's kids. Vases were broken and paintings slashed. The rental Steinway upright had marijuana burns and Bud Light stains, the refrigerator had scary things growing out of Styrofoam cups and stank like the river Styx, and miscellaneous debris was ankle-deep. I called 1-800-GOT-JUNK and asked them to bring a dumpster in the morning.

Quite weary, Gayle and I gave each other a quick hug and bedded down in pajamas on opposite sides of my queen-sized bed. At her insistence we planned to attend a lecture on black holes and avocado toast by Neil deGrasse Tyson the following day.

In the morning, after nightmares of being shot at, we lay in bed while the Got Junk crew did its thing. I authorized them to throw anything into the dumpster they deemed junk, and not to disturb us with questions. We were tired and muttered distractedly on our backs about our residency in Cyprus.

You may have noticed that as narrator I've rarely presumed to access psychic interiors on my own but have mostly let my principals, including Rimbaud, reveal themselves. Even with these revelations, the various attractions or aversions among the fellows have eluded full explanation. I do have access to my own interior and remind you that I had never been in love.

When the way was clear in the late afternoon, Gayle and I climbed out of bed, made strong coffee, and showered separately. She downed her cocktail, and we headed off to John's of Bleecker Street, where we ordered a large pizza with sausage, meatballs, pepperoni, garlic, onion, bell peppers, mushrooms, ricotta, anchovies, olives, roasted heirloom tomatoes in olive oil, fresh basil, and extra mozzarella. Also lots of oregano, cracked red pepper, and grated Parmesan. Then it was time to head off to the American Museum of Natural History on Central Park West, known as the Teddy Roosevelt museum because the great conservationist filled dioramas with personally slaughtered beasts. Within the museum's walls was the Rose Center for Earth and Space, where Neil deGrasse Tyson would be speaking.

"My parents brought me here when I was a little girl," said Gayle upon our exiting the subway at 77th Street. "It's what made me decide to be a scientist. I love it!"

With his expressive hand gestures even more whelming than usual, Tyson concluded that avocado toast within black holes cannot be ruled out because information leaks out of black holes very slowly, if ever. We joined others in a standing ovation and headed for the passageway that leads to the heart of the museum.

"Melusina had a great idea when she hid in Saint Hilarion's castle to look for Aphrodite's treasure," said Gayle, who had heard of this transgression after she returned from Turkey. "Let's do it here and stay all night. What's the big deal? They let kids stay overnight."

"Carefully supervised by adults," I said, being more cautious in all matters than Gayle.

"We *are* adults. When that guard isn't looking, run down the hall to the North American Mammals. It's nine o'clock and most of the staff has gone home."

Without waiting for my consent, Gayle flew birdlike through the passageway, her L.L.Bean cargo vest flapping, and I gamely followed, less bird than jackass. She ran ahead and I lumbered after. There we were, after hours at the Museum of Natural History. Now what?

Inside the hall of North American Mammals, the overhead lights were turned off but the dioramas were dimly lit, making for an eerie display of stuffed animals who, for all I knew, would come back to life after hours.

Breathing hard, terrified, and unaccustomed to physical exertion, I managed an intelligent question. "Gayle, do you know what we have in common with these beasts?"

"Yup, we're North American mammals too. You more than I, being from farther north. Let's do as many dioramas as possible until dawn. These aren't as scary as the African mammals that Teddy bagged but still worth a look. The really scary stuff is the dinosaurs on the fourth floor. They're not behind protective glass."

In the hall of dioramas we snuck up on the Canadian bighorn sheep, the Arizonan mountain goat, and the Alaskan dall sheep— each in a realistic habitat—for they reminded us uncannily of mouflon. Cyprus is sadly underrepresented in this otherwise great museum, but we made imaginative connections. I say *snuck up* because these animals all seemed so real they would surely flee if we startled them.

Gayle took my hand. "Bart, are you still spooked? They're not as bad as the impersonators."

"I feel we're being watched. They're looking at us as if we're invaders. Remember, you're a scientist but I'm a humanist and get easily spooked."

Gayle squeezed my hand harder and I worried that I might get trigger thumb just as she had given me close to a meniscus tear in the Cessna. But I also warmed to that hand. Have you seen the image of the human body that indicates through proportional distortion how much of the human brain is engaged in controlling any particular part? The hand is monstrous. Holding hands engages more of our brains than having sex.

We decided to seek out more exotic beasts so went upstairs, hand in hand, to the Hall of African Mammals where we encountered at the center a pack of eight African elephants not caged and ready to defend territory. The dim light somehow made them all the more likely to stampede. "We come as friends," I said, truly nervous.

"Bart, you're ridiculous. Come visit my favorite animals. Darcy would envy us, except that, well, let's face it, these animals are all dead, really dead. It's not a zoo for endangered species."

"I'm not so sure they're dead. You go first."

We visited the dioramas of the Kalahari black wildebeest, the Mozambique cheetah, the Tanzania greater kudu, and the Lake Victoria impala. They were mesmerizing, but it was the Kivu mountain gorilla beating its chest who made the greatest claim.

"We're looking at an early version of ourselves," said Gayle.

"I've read my Stephen Jay Gould and know that evolution doesn't imply improvement. It's random. Some species luck out, others drop out. There was nothing inevitable about humans emerging or surviving. Is it undiplomatic to say that there can even be a decline? Maybe we're exceptions, but it seems to me that human beings are a falling away from this gorilla."

"Gotta agree with you, Bart. Gorillas fight for territory but not to the death, and there's no record of a gorilla civil war or a gorilla as dumb as President—I can't say his name."

Gayle and I were getting along in the dim luminescence of the closed museum. Would we be this much in sync within other habitats?

"Let's go visit the dinosaurs," she said with ardor. "There are so many new ones since I was here as a girl. Dinosaurs no longer schlump along. Some of them are like lemurs and come in rainbow colors."

"And tasty. Those songbirds are dinosaurs. We're eating dinosaurs when we order chicken."

"So well informed for a humanist! You've read C. P. Snow on the 'two cultures'? Scientists and humanists oughta learn from one another. Maybe *we* should!"

I let these words hang in silence as we made our way to the fourth floor and beheld the ancestors of birds, the saurischian dinosaurs. There stood a Tyrannosaurus rex.

"What does this theropod have in common with Kentucky Fried Chicken?" I asked, trying to be witty but truly not knowing.

"If you wanna know, I can tell you. Chickens and Rex here share a pubis that points downward and forward at an angle to the ischium. Every fifth-grader knows that."

"Seems to me they're too young to hear about a pubis, but I'll let that go."

What I didn't let go was Gayle herself. By the end of a week of adventures much like this one, all her doing, I was for the first time in my life totally in love. She had made her way like a haunting to a core I didn't know was there. We proposed simultaneously under the Washington Square Arch. Before she flew to California, we went down to City Hall and got married. Reluctantly taking an Uber from the Upper East Side, Albert and a passerby served as witnesses. Our marriage was consummated by a kiss, a hug, and a handshake, for we knew we would be forever sex-free, by choice, not fear. Being sex-free appealed to both of us for different reasons. It's a bit more complicated, but Gayle had lived so long without that she'd lost all craving and preferred flying to fucking. You've heard enough about my own sorry sex life to know that I'd have little regret in saying goodbye to the sorrows of Priapus. We could have fiery love without coupling, valuing one another for our essential selves and being happy with hugs.

We wore gold rings found in a Bleecker Street pawnshop. As a midlist author I couldn't afford a diamond of any magnitude, and anyway we had skipped the engagement ordeal.

After Gayle did her semester gig at Davis, flying back solo to the city every other weekend, she took a job as clinical assistant professor of meteorology at NYU, where she could teach on and off. We moved to a larger apartment, at 23 Bank Street, between former residences of Willa Cather and Bella Abzug.

Gayle begins every day with her cocktail and I with my antidepressant black coffee, crouched over a manuscript. With my Paper Mate #2 Sharpwriter, I scribble on yellow legal pads, feeling a warmer intimacy with my fabrications than a computer could yield. Our careers have proved symbiotic. As you know, I live for travel and adventure, and she knows how to fly, improving on her skills in learning how to dodge drones. As we figure-eight and upside-down our way to distant ports of call where I can absorb the ambient culture and write yet another midlist memoir, she makes her meteorological measurements and continues the Al Gore anti-apocalypse campaign with fresh data on carbon emissions, global warming, and cow flatulence.

Albert Vygotsky won two Nobel prizes in 2027—sort of. The Estonians withdrew their objections when it was discovered they had fabricated their charge of fabrication as a way of getting greater academic visibility and another chance at tenure. Ignoring a 4:00 a.m. phone call interrupting a sweet dream that he was getting a 4:00 a.m. phone call from Stockholm, Albert later opened his computer to the *New York Times* news summary, read the headline, and sullenly announced to his Cheshire cat, already biting at his ankles for breakfast: "Some American *alter kaker* has won the Nobel Prize in medicine." He put on his bifocals and read more closely, crying out to Toby, "*I'm* the *alter kaker!*" But when he returned the phone call that had, sure enough, come from Stockholm, the Nobel Prize receptionist told him that because he had not picked up they had given the award to the two first runners-up, according to newly instituted protocols following the Bob Dylan debacle.

A week later he ignored a 4:00 a.m. phone call interrupting another sweet dream that he was getting a 4:00 a.m. phone call, this time from Oslo. Same deal. It was the Peace Prize, always awarded by the Norwegians instead of the Swedes. Because he had not picked up, they had no choice but to go down their list.

I feel that Albert was right to object and take his brief to the World Court at The Hague, which had tired of failed war-crime trials and was adjudicating lesser offenses. After much debate they decided in his favor, but he had to share the booty.

After an ordeal of righteous indignation, Albert renounced the profession of science and resigned his professorship at Rockefeller. Nobel hopefuls now sit next to their landlines all the night through during prize-announcement weeks. Loss of a week's sleep, sometimes two, has diminished the productivity of these geniuses.

You ask about Darcy? Because of his success with sea turtles, mouflon, and *ambelopoúlia*, he was appointed director of the Gerald Durrell Zoo in Jersey, England. Like Durrell, he was childfree but certainly not free of his own kind of progeny, for like Durrell he was opposed to zoos as animal prisons for jeering child spectators. He favored them as breeding grounds for endangered species. As of this writing he has bred in captivity the Bulmer's fruit bat, the Rio Pescado stubfoot toad, the Pygmy three-toed sloth, Nelson's small-eared shrew, the Sumatran rhino, and the Table Mountain ghost frog.

The latter has the distinction of being invisible, so some naturalists object to its being placed on the most-endangered list. Like dark matter we could be enmeshed in these goddam ghost frogs and never know it.

Apparently, Darcy has somewhat modified his brash personality and is said to be an avuncular presence within his menagerie. A recent photograph shows a smiling corpulent late-middle-aged man confronting a huge plate of chips, the grease of which he is cutting through with an unmistakable bottle of zivanía.

The Rimbaud impersonator died of bone cancer at the age of thirty-seven. The Gerald Durrell impersonator died of septicemia following a liver transplant at the age of seventy. The Lawrence Durrell impersonator died of a stroke while on the potty at the age of seventy-eight. The William Shakespeare impersonator died a suicide by poison at the age of fifty-two.

If it is any consolation to them and us, all were members of Actors Equity and received fairly prominent obits in the *New York Digital Times*. Requiescat in pace.

EPILOGUE

In August of 2030, I called for a reunion of the Cyprus Think Tank, held in a singular venue, the Oneida Community Mansion House in upstate New York. I asked Soros to rent the entire ninety-three-thousand-square-foot complex—a nineteenth-century Italianate phantasmagoria in red brick with high-ceilinged guest rooms, two well-stocked libraries, many assembly rooms, ornate cupolas, and on its grounds the world's largest walnut and tulip trees.

Sustained immaculately as a landmark by the state of New York, the Mansion House has few overnight visitors because the joint is said to be haunted. The Oneida Community was founded by a religious fanatic, one John Humphrey Noyes, and practiced "Bible Communism," best known for polyamory. Not exactly free love, because Noyes and an inner circle decided who could have an "interview" with whom. Noyes disinterestedly took upon himself the deflowering of all pubescent girls. Because God commands us to love one another equally, a corollary was that "sticky love," or possessiveness and jealousy, was forbidden as unholy. At one point he felt the young girls were themselves exhibiting sticky love toward their dolls, so he forced them to line up and sacrifice the dolls in a corncob stove. Some have uncharitably thought the motive behind Noyes's Christian spirituality was an over-the-top testosterone level and need of cover for his rampant promiscuity. Kinder observers applaud his impartiality in having sired thirteen children by thirteen different women.

John Humphrey Noyes initiated the only eugenics program ever in the United States, beating out Hitler by some seven decades. He and a central committee decided which Oneida residents had qualities worthy of perpetuation in a protocol called stirpiculture. Though many applicants were turned down, fifty-eight stirps were bred by the late 1870s, all of them quite ordinary.

Whatever scruples one might have about polyamory and eugenics, the Oneida Community was the most successful utopian experiment ever in America, not only building the most impressive edifice but also out-performing competitors as the world's largest maker of iron animal traps, silken thread, and Oneidan Community silverware—the world's most famous brand, which guaranteed in glossy advertising that for World War II soldiers there was something worth returning home to besides welcoming arms.

So why, you may be asking, hold a reunion of the Cyprus Think Tank in such a place? One answer is, why not? The labyrinthine corridors, secret passageways, and high ornamental ceilings make for great fun. Hide-and-seek could go on forever. And given the scientific bent of most of us, its spookiness was a psycho-aesthetic thrill we didn't often indulge.

More so, we admitted to a utopian impulse, if in different degrees, and the Cyprus Think Tank, let's face it, had been an experiment in utopianism. Could we learn from the Oneidans? What had we learned about ourselves? For Melusina, the Mansion House was a good fit, a reminder of how she had once orchestrated her love life. You can't visit the Oneida Community Mansion House without thinking about sex, and sex has maintained a low but persistent hum throughout my story.

We assembled in the second-floor amphitheater, which featured representations on its ceiling of the classical Muses instead of Christian angels, and a stage where *HMS Pinafore* was performed by community musicians and singers in 1879. In this amphitheater Oneidans gathered for weekly "criticism" sessions that anticipated the encounter groups of the seventies. Everyone was dressed down by the larger group for character flaws. I thought it better not to ape the brutality of the Oneidan Community and seventies' encounter groups, but something might be gained in having each of us get on stage and bring the group up to date. What had we done the past six years and did we remember the Cyprus Think Tank with affection or shame? We could ask any question and make observations in the spirit of friendly dialogue.

Melusina mounted the stage first, barefoot and in her white toga with purple stripe. "Bart, we've waited around six years now for your Cyprus memoir," she began. "Why the delay? You've published two others in the meantime."

"Nobody would believe a word of it," I said. "And I've had trouble sorting it all out—a mingled yarn. What did we learn? Tell me, I'll write. I was keeping a notebook and can fact-check."

"One thing I learned is that polyamory was good for a time but same-sex monogamy is a better addiction now. Jasmine and I have the stickiest love imaginable."

Jasmine smiled and nodded. "We improve on the Oneidans and Noyes. The very idea of same-sex sex made that pervert want to barf."

"But what of archeology and your great find, the Aphrodite of Pygmalion? We have our fingers crossed."

"*Verdammt!* Had to be a powerful helicopter to steal her. Emperor Putin is still the prime suspect, you know. I hope she isn't once again underwater—getting her out wasn't easy. She is probably locked into a Kremlin vault the dork visits every day to show off his disgusting pecs and worship her backside. That's after his morning sauna and fresh round of executions. I've done well by her and she'll turn up again someday. Archeologists take a long view of things. I'm still working the lost cities of Africa, thanks to Jasmine. As soon as we're finished with Cameroon, we'll find another African site and start digging. Meanwhile, we've all heard that the economy of

Western Cyprus is taking a hit. Hotel reservations in Páphos made last year are being canceled. Aphrodite was the main draw—that backside you know."

"Speaking of the economy," I put in, "I guess we overestimated the long-term effect of the Venetian gold." I was thinking of the island's economic disaster after the national bank handed out mortgages to all applicants, whether they had means or not. Now there was forty percent unemployment, houses and hotels falling into disrepair, even casinos going out of business. The prostitutes of Limassol had lowered their rates just to make ends meet. Armide and Renaud were hoisted out of office by a military coup and are exiled in Argentina, where they don't speak the language. Word is they still haven't learned each other's.

"But this doesn't mean the discovery of the gold was for nothing," put in Jasmine. "Cyprus briefly enjoyed a rebirth. Nothing is forever."

"We writers like to think we are forever, our works, that is. We live on in them. Shakespeare said so in his sonnets, and who am I to disagree?"

"Why was he a suicide then?" asked Albert.

"The Muse deserted him after the Globe burned. For three years he hung around his humdrum hometown. Couldn't write anything after *The Tempest*, and suicide is the most efficient cure for depression. Better than waiting around for bone cancer or septicemia or a stroke. Funny that nobody else has ever guessed this. Now Albert, how have you spent the past few years, having won then lost then won two Nobels?"

Albert shuffled to the stage. "*Oy*, angry, depressed, also disappointed. Have you noticed the nations still furiously rage together?"

"Yes, why is that? Your Empathomax was supposed to make even politicians have empathy. The divorce rate of Greek and Turkish couples has soared lately. What happened, or didn't?"

"*Oy vey*, nobody could replicate my results. That's what science is all about. The Nobel Committee thinks they were right to deny me the prizes in the first place because my work turns out to have been crap. Some schnook just got a Nobel for proving I was even wronger than anybody said. I'll never know why it worked in Cyprus for a season."

"But how do you feel, really *feel*, about your defeat?" asked Jasmine from the front row. "Do you feel defeated, Albert? And how do you feel about this schnook? Resentment? Or maybe it's just a letdown? Let us know how you feel, dude." Jasmine had been listening to old Terry Gross podcasts.

"I don't *feel* anything, I just shifted gears. Haven't you heard? I'm now a standup comic as an Albert Vygotsky impersonator. I didn't need to undergo a name change. I'm one of only a handful of standup comics with two Nobel prizes. Everything I say makes people laugh. I have no idea why, I'm not trying . . . it just seems I'm funny. I use the words *fuck* and *dick* a lot. Never used them before except in Yiddish, but after I quit Rockefeller I took a course in standup comedy at the NYU Tisch School of the Arts, and they told me to say *fuck* and *dick* all the time. Dick jokes are where it's at, they said. I also pull out my Yiddish. Everybody laughs even though they don't know Yiddish. Those dickheads. Why the fuck?"

Sure enough, we all laughed. The question this raised was the perennial one: Can people genuinely change or is there a bedrock in our personality that abides? Now a professional humorist, Albert was still a grouch and for that we were grateful.

Jasmine took the stage next. She had put on some weight. "Tackled my anorexia if only so I wouldn't be crushed by Melusina during our embraces." We laughed. "The Oneidans shifted from having 'interviews' to making bourgeois silverware—triple-plated and not sterling—and I shifted from not eating to eating—and real food. Melusina brings me the world's best chocolate every day of the year, real chocolate all the way through."

"How do you compete now with the author of *The Cave Woman's Diet*?" I asked diplomatically, knowing that authors of best sellers are often perplexed about what to write next.

"Easy. *The Cave Woman's Diet Redux* comes out in the spring," replied Jasmine. "It's being adapted for the movies, but how you turn a cookbook into a movie is anybody's guess."

"Do you ever miss men?" asked Darcy, an un-PC question but one that had occurred to me also.

"That would be like missing haggis, you know, the disgusting Scottish goulash made in the stomach of a dead sheep. You're a vegetarian, maybe you get the point, Darcy."

"*The Cave Woman's Diet* lost traction in Cyprus after the new Minister of the Interior reinstated chips," observed Melusina. "And with the loss of Aphrodite, out went the paradigm for the New Woman on that island."

We sighed.

"So, Darcy," I asked, "what's the latest on your zoo? And please remind us of the long-range consequences of your many triumphs in Cyprus."

He mounted the stage with difficulty, given his biomass. "It's a little sad. The mouflon so overpopulated the island that a bounty was declared and bloody hunters went to work hauling in horns to collect euros. Their high testosterone made the horns great aphrodisiacs when ground to smithereens. Three times more effective than Viagra. How could I have known?"

"It's called moral luck," I said, "which means moral *bad* luck. We can only guess at consequences."

"What about the sea turtles?" asked Melusina.

"The sea level has risen so much that the new elevation levels we taught the critters aren't high enough. Their hatchlings are drowning. Bloody tourists still put on virtual-reality goggles, so that's survived, but it's *virtual* reality, not reality."

"And the songbirds?" asked Albert. "Never ate a songbird I didn't like. Fuck! Dick!"

Nobody laughed.

"All those fake songbirds donated by the Soros foundation have long ago been swallowed, and Cypriots caught on that they were fakes. So they're back laying traps. It's patriotic. But I'm dead chuffed about my zoo. They copulate like animals! With a chips addiction, nothing I can do about my waistline. Please Jasmine, you've been an addict—to not eating—some sympathy please. They say that men with big bread baskets don't last long." Darcy sighed. He looked mortal.

"Gayle, you're up next. We all know what happened with your rainmaking formula . . ."

Gayle fairly flew to the stage but her report was a downer. "Yup, who would have thought that hydrochlorothiazide would cause acid rain, right? The perverts call it Gayle's Golden Showers. This phrase is forever my claim to fame, according to Wikipedia. Well, the rain did have a golden sheen . . . I never guessed it *was* part urine! You've probably heard the sequel. At first the grass and crops perked up but as acid made its way into the stamens and pistols, they shriveled. So Cyprus, Turkey, the Sahara, California— you name it—they're the worse off for Gayle's Golden Showers. The Soros foundation found some environmental lawyers to ward off suits and keep me out of jail."

"Sad. But what about you and Bart? How's that going?" asked Melusina, never hesitating to ask relationship questions.

"Fine, we're totally compatible. I fly him wherever and monitor air currents. Remember, I'm a meteorologist and study the thing nobody else is any good at—the weather. I had a setback in those golden showers, but Al Gore tells me this is a temporary inconvenience. Like everybody else after Hillary's big goof, he doesn't send me emails anymore—his tidings come by personal messenger on rollerblades. Right now, I'm funneling cow flatulence into a sustainable energy source to make fracking obsolete. Mind you, don't ask during dinner about the funneling process."

Everybody laughed, and Gayle looked down at me for a nod that she could become more confessional. "Bart and I have no sticky love to gum things up and no risk of producing stirps. We're childfree. Come to think of it, nobody here is good at producing stirps. The human stock will enjoy no boost from us, and Hobbes may get the last words—our lives are 'solitary, poor, nasty, brutish, and short.' Thank you, Mister Hobbes, now go away."

"Don't wish to disagree with you, spouse, but I wish to disagree."

I took the stage. I'd been taking stock of what my colleagues were saying, also absorbing the Mansion House itself, its history and meaning. To judge by my oratory, I should have been a Rotarian instead of a memoirist. "The Oneidans had a utopian impulse," I began, "but one anchored in religion and Noyes's notion of amative activity free of sticky love. Heaven promised an eternity of angelic orgasm, so why not get a head start? Humans might as well get good practice for what would be an eternal second coming in two senses. Jesus enjoined us to fuck our brains out here on earth, or so Noyes thought, but in a way that didn't lift merely human attachments above love of God. The result at Oneida was a productive community founded on total lunacy. Sticky love eventually caught up with them, but they had a good ride."

The fellows nodded, so I went on, with hand gestures not unlike those of Neil deGrasse Tyson.

"Our Cyprus Think Tank had its own utopian impulse founded not in supernaturalism but secular enlightened notions of social engineering. We made a checklist of the problems troubling a small island. For a time it seemed we were achieving all our goals and could hope to export our wisdom elsewhere, just as the Oneidans set up subsidiaries in Canadian Niagara Falls and Brooklyn.

"Fellow think tankers—my great tanks, er, thanks for accepting my invitation to this reunion. So far it isn't maudlin. Before we go for dinner in the banquet room, pillow fights in our bedrooms, and ghost sightings of Oneidans and the thousands of poor animals killed by their traps, I'd like to offer some reflections on our brief time together in Cyprus and what lies ahead . . . Yes, our remedies worked for a time but didn't take—and Cyprus, once again, is an island beset by woe. It remains a microcosm of what besets the human race at this moment in the twenty-first century."

I looked down at the fellows to make sure they weren't getting the fidgets. I then came to the heart of the matter. "We now know the proximate cause of our setbacks—those damned dragonflies! Darcy, with all due respect, why couldn't you see that they were robots? If only you had let Albert go ahead and swat one that day at the Chelidonia! Then we'd have known it had gears, not guts."

"Bloody sorry about that, but they would have fooled Darwin."

"Okay, you're forgiven, sort of. With your permission, fellows, I'll rehearse what we now know. The CIA began concocting the Insectothopter in the seventies. The surveillance drone couldn't navigate crosswinds. But the Trump creeps put it back on track, modeled on a species more drab and less conspicuous than others."

"Yes! I'd have caught on to *Anax imperator*, who is larger and more colorful. His gearbox would have made more of a racket."

"These fake bugs monitored our every move," I continued. "They served the collective will of Trump's CIA, the right-wing Turkish government, and Putin. These fakes brought together superpowers often at odds."

"Yup, real mischief, but the dragonflies didn't make my formula produce urine rain," said Gayle.

"Okay, but they did enough, tipping off the Turkish air force to intercept your Cessna. They blocked all our electronic devices so we wouldn't know a tsunami was coming our way. They supplied precise specs on the Aphrodite of Pygmalion so Putin could make a move on her. They manipulated Armide and Renaud into marriage and a duumvirate of the dumb that insured incompetent leadership across the island, bringing on a terrible recession despite the Venetian gold. They fed our *Othello* fiasco to social media and subjected us to global ridicule. And they usurped the radio stations of Limassol to spread the rumor of a collapsing songbird economy. I must say, for mere dragonflies they spoke admirable Greek and Turkish, if with an irritating timbre."

"Never underestimate dragonflies, Bart," warned Darcy.

"With respect, I'd like to put farce aside for a moment and ask what this tragedy has meant. Back in 2022 I conceived a simple plot—let's gang up on Cyprus and fix it. We conquered this, then that, like adolescents on a joyride. Yes, we had our subplots as some of us hankered after others... Nice that some of these infatuations have borne fruit. But we didn't know what the real plot was—a larger plot against us undertaken by powers of darkness, anchored in fatuity and bigotry. The unseen plot became the real plot and sank our think tank. Do humans ever know the real plot that engulfs them?"

Darcy and Albert began stomping their feet to indicate I should bring my oration to a close. Dinner was waiting.

"I'll be quick. There's something at the heart of international diplomacy that abhors utopian vision. Inveterate enemies can unite against it, an affront to realpolitik, as Henry Kissinger would insist. There's a chorus of deniers chanting 'Don't tell us to dream of a better world. War and poverty are as human as hemorrhoids, flat feet, and male pattern baldness.'"

"Are you talking about me?" asked Albert. "Kindly desist."

"We still don't know the motive behind the launch of those damn dragonflies," I continued. "Seems to have been a hidden convergence of evil forces deeper than anything imagined by Shakespeare or Rimbaud. It was the ultimate deaf ear to what Schiller said about how politics must pass through the gut of the aesthetic to reach beauty and freedom."

"Go Schiller!" cried Melusina.

"Mister Midlist Beasley, it will never happen and you're slow to vacate the stage," complained Darcy. "Let's eat!"

"One minute more... Let's not all give up. I'm happy to announce that a second group of geniuses, inspired by us and again financed by the Soros foundation, will be setting up headquarters in Nicosia next year. A chemist among them is at work to find a substitute for hydrochlorothiazide that will be productive of rain wholly void, er, *devoid* of urine. A city planner has a master plan to rehabilitate all crumbling structures, do away with urban blight, and restore to all major cities the grandeur of ancient Salamis, without its downside of human and animal sacrifice. A couples counselor with a track record in magnet therapy will reunite marriages where ethnic hatred has again fostered early morning homicides. An engineer has proposed a way of lifting strategic beaches a few meters so they cannot be overtaken by the rising sea level. Word has it that he is inspired by something he read in *Gulliver's Travels*. And there are four or five other specialists who will help out with problems we didn't even consider. They will be on the lookout for robotic dragonflies and have already devised a steel mesh net. You get the picture? We were only one stage in the evolution of the island and must now yield to others."

There was anemic applause from my coterie of seasoned, damaged geniuses. "Yes, one think tank must give way to another, to echo Shakespeare, Keats, and Tennyson." They could rely on me for learned allusion. I went on. "One item that worked out was Rimbaud's notebook—the magenta *Cahier II*. Though some Rimbaud scholars still doubt its authenticity, I had it auctioned at Sotheby's for a bundle, as you know—twenty-five million bucks less the fifty percent commission Sotheby's took for having an auctioneer hold the notebook up for a few minutes. The winning bid came from an anonymous bidder in Dubai, some say a Trump crony long in exile to escape jail. It's been tucked somewhere. But I managed to transcribe and translate the whole thing into seven languages before it disappeared into a private vault. I've donated half the money to antiquity preservation on Cyprus and lots to the Soros foundation by way of thanks for its behind-the-scenes support over the years. I've retained just enough to pay for Gayle's morning cocktails and an upgraded set of seat belts for our Cessna." Polite laughter.

"How's your literary career, Bart?" asked Jasmine abruptly, with a certain insensitivity to the plight of authors. "Are you still midlisted? Haven't seen anything by you at the Strand, but came across a couple of memoirs at a garage sale in Yaoundé—so you must be getting around."

"The concept of *midlist* has been trashed, Jasmine, and the whole notion of *the book* has been under assault from recto to verso, so there can be no in-between, as in the lamentable term *midlist*, a euphemism for *don't bother*. It's dominated my sorry literary life. And there are no longer backlists in the publishing industry, only debris fields in gutted New Jersey warehouses, routinely burned down by publishers to collect insurance. University libraries have been commandeered by students looking into computer screens and never taking a book down from the stacks.

"Even so I scribble as an aspirant in life's human comedy, hoping my little books will go forth and prosper. We six share this as hangers-on in a post-human world. We are flawed and endangered in various ways—our health, our sanity, our luck and lack of it. But when we joined the Cyprus Think Tank we shared an admirable pluck in rescuing the Aphrodite, the songbirds and mouflon, the sea turtles, agriculture, public health, the Venetian gold, the House of Durrell as a cultural institution, and Rimbaud's notebook. We were trying to shape the world according to our best imaginings—the end of ethnic hatred, desertification, chips. That we were nearly tarred and feathered for our good deeds is in keeping with the morass of human history, if one remembers the likes of Jesus, Bruno, Galileo, Martin Luther King, and Benazir Bhutto. No reading more depressing than large-scale histories of civilization. What we know of ancient Rome is benighted emperors, battles, assassinations, slavery, gladiatorial combat, whoring, pederasty, and never collecting the garbage. This is in no way to fault the Cypriots, for they did what humans have always done, and our scheme did smack of an outsider's presumption. Let's hope the second think tank has better luck."

"Stop it, Bart, you're depressing the bejesus out of us," cried Darcy.

"Thanks, I needed that. Because what I meant to say is that as hardy aspirants in life's human comedy we stuck together—sometimes with sticky love—and did our best to rescue an island as disinterested practitioners of our skills. I confess to having had the least disinterested of motives. My dreamworld had gone flat and I needed good material for another memoir. But the thrust of our think tank has buoyed me up and sustained us all. Maybe someday a round blue plaque in the best British tradition will be hung on one of the houses we occupied in Káthikas, not unlike the signage for Rimbaud's hunting lodge in the Tróödos. 'Here, in 2024, the Great Cyprus Think Tank lived and devised plans for the betterment of this island. It cannot be said that they did not try.'" Muted applause again as Gayle, weeping, helped me down from the stage.

We adjourned to the banquet awaiting us in the principal library—a voluminous chamber with skylights through which the Milky Way rolled on. The library itself was encyclopedic—an homage to print culture, with hardcover first editions going back to the mid-nineteenth century. One could find all the novels of Thackeray, Dickens, Hardy, Tolstoy, Cather, and Proust, and the great nonfiction, the natural histories of von Humboldt, Darwin, and H.G. Wells. On the banquet table were the choice edibles of Cyprus, flown in by the Soros foundation. We scarfed them down with the dry red wine of Káthikas, making toasts and dancing the celebratory Cypriot *syrtos*. Even Albert did a kind of animated shuffle and performed one of his deadpan standups, which had us all clutching guts. We were happy.

That night, in sumptuous room 141, with Gayle in a chaste spoon position, I dreamt a dream—a most delicious dream. I dreamt the six of us were in Gayle's Cessna as we rapidly ascended from Páphos airport. Again we viewed the Akámas peninsula to the northwest, the Tróödos mountains to the northeast, and the Kyrenian range beyond them. We beheld distant Famagusta and the ruins of Salamis.

But something was different. Everything was green. Cyprus had become an oasis. Then I knew that the second think tank had succeeded where we failed. We passed over the isle of Yeronisos, and there she was, standing stately and callipygian, the Aphrodite of

Pygmalion, rescued once again. Melusina wept. As we neared Cape Lára we could see a wide sandy beach. Had it been raised? Darcy exclaimed that he could see Beulah the loggerhead clambering up the beach to lay her eggs yet again. The Akámas peninsula was overgrown with vines and pines. Was that Aphrodite locked in a carnal embrace with Adonis within a lush garden? So I beheld, and there was no counter-evidence. As we neared the Tróödos, a herd of mouflon scampered while Darcy watched with his binoculars. "There's Bragadino!" he cried with joy. "Way to go, pal!"

Passing over the Governor's Lodge, I saw the slender form of Rimbaud, who looked up at us with his irradiate blue eyes. Smiling, he waved and I waved back with a sense of the fellowship of writers. Then to the House of Durrell in Béllapais, with the Tree of Idleness standing firm, and somehow I could see Durrell himself at his desk, writing *Justine* while drinking zivanía and smoking a Gitane. I could even read the words of his manuscript: *I have escaped to this island with a few books and the child—Melissa's child. I do not know why I use the word escape. The villagers say jokingly that only a sick man would choose such a remote place to rebuild. Well then, I have come here to heal myself, if you like to put it that way . . .*

I felt these words entering my writer's brain, enlivening it. I could write anything now. As we flew over Famagusta we beheld the aristocratic form of lovely Desdemona, spared the sticky love of Othello and restored to life, as immortal as Shakespeare himself. I knew that Cyprus was now a peaceable kingdom, its factions healed, its antiquities restored, its land bountiful and life-giving.

I awakened with a start and Gayle asked me if I was dreaming. "A dream maybe," I said, "but I prefer to believe it."

A sneak peek at Larry Lockridge's upcoming novel

Out of Wedlock

Jess Freeman, a facial plastic surgeon who refashions the identities of others, knows little of his own identity. Who are his biological parents and could they be the source of his sudden trances, when he drifts off into visionary worlds, by turns radiant and nightmarish? Reality checks—quick bops on his head—are administered by his nurse during delicate surgeries. But fumbling Jess pulls off a superb makeover of a severely injured patient, which leads to striking revelations. Through Greenwich Village and Santa Fe from 1989 to 2008, Jess's romantic misadventures echo perils of the heart endured in the salad days of Edna St. Vincent Millay and D. H. Lawrence, the sexual revolution of the sixties and seventies, and today's hookup generation. But Jess and his close companions more than endure; whatever their fates, they are sustained by a group loyalty anchored in pluck, buoyancy, and affection.

— Chapter One —

BONES WHO DANCE

The skeletons, cracking vertebrae and knuckles as they emerged from the ground, were a vision in yellow. Jess remembered that eighteenth- and nineteenth-century victims of yellow fever, buried in Washington Square, were wrapped in yellow sheets. A few skeletons, in penitentials, had been cut down from the hangman's tree at the northwest corner. He could see fractures in the cervical vertebrae. Odd—some were sporting erections, but he knew that hominids aren't armed with penis bones.

The small clavicles of one executed offender suggested a female. This could be Rose, the young Black woman hanged in 1819 for suspected arson. She was the last to be hanged in Washington Square, which then became a military parade ground.

There were twenty-one thousand stiffs here, mostly potter's-field types. About two hundred pushed through the sod, stood upright, and began assembling close to Washington Square Arch, as if at a demo. Except they were all grinning.

Jess approached from the south as the skeletons tramped rhythmically northward and surrounded the arch. He began to sweat, for creepier than these skeletons were the two marble statues of George Washington who descended from their pediments on the arch. With slow and ponderous steps, they pushed through the encirclement of bones and set up for their gig. One carried a synthesizer, the other a set of drums.

During a recent renovation of the arch, both underwent extreme makeovers. Jess had often passed the Georges, noting how the prominent chins were weathering away, the cheeks flattening, and the lower faces displaying an embarrassing soft-tissue descent. What a challenge the Georges presented! Jess hoped the restorers wouldn't later be slapped with malpractice suits.

The makeovers seemed to have gone to the Georges' heads. What music should eighteenth- and nineteenth-century skeletons expect of them? An allemande? A minuet? A gigue? Certainly not the fusion of reggae, electro-industrial heavy metal, post-bop doo-wop, and neo-garage mojo that cleared the park of rats and pigeons. Their huge forms swayed before the arch as they competed in miking up higher and higher.

Jess felt sorry for the skeletons. They didn't know how to dance to heavy metal or neo-garage mojo. They assumed an early American formation, the longways line, male skeletons facing female, joining phalanges and metacarpals in groups of four and changing couples up and down the line. The music didn't fit, so they stumbled over one another in this dance of death, falling on the cobblestones, breaking their bones.

But after a few more minutes of deafening trash fusion, they caught on. Sternums scraped against sternums, sacra pressed against sacra, female femurs spread apart to give intimate access to one partner after another. Jess beheld a frenzy of skeletal coupling—females with males, females with females, males with males, sturdy skeletons with decrepit. A few skeletal dogs entered in, adding to the mix.

The bronze statue of Garibaldi, deliverer of Italy, strode over to find out what was going on and averted his eyes.

As a kid, Jess had learned to make a fire by rubbing twigs together. That may explain what happened next. As the skeletons humped one another and piled up like World Series champs, catastrophe was near. All at once, a feverish threesome auto-ignited near the bottom, and a conflagration spread through the heap of pathetically groping, delirious bones. A bonfire towered over Washington Square Arch, showering sparks into the empyrean. Jess panicked as the fire was engulfing him, bringing with it a mélange of partially incinerated metatarsals, fibula, tibia, and grinning toothy mandibles.

He screamed and woke up. He was not alone.

Out of Wedlock is the third novel in *The Enigma Quartet*, following *The Cardiff Giant* and *The Great Cyprus Think Tank*. The fourth novel, *The Woman in Green*, will be released in 2022.

CPSIA information can be obtained
at www.ICGtesting.com
Printed in the USA
LVHW101747300322
714841LV00019B/509/J

9 781771 804974